A Compelling Novel

THE TROUBLE WITH AVA

Stuart Friedman

Author of THE WAY WE LOVE and
THE REVOLT OF JILL BRADDOCK

I0554252

WILDSIDE PRESS

THE TROUBLE WITH AVA

For
Jeannette

One

It was five A.M. and still dark outside. Inside the Fourleaf Club there was fluorescent daylight, toneless except for the occasional twitching of a defective tube. Most of the games were shut down; a mop crew worked in a roped-off section. A few sleeepless walkers and watchers trickled in and out of the big casino without playing. Tired clerks at the Keeno counter stared vacantly at a few nearly motionless old men waiting around with marked slips for the next drawing. A house shill wearing a work glove and pulling three levers in a steady, dismal rhythm was the only player on the long lines of slot machines. The play at the craps table, at one of two open blackjack deals and at the lone operating roulette wheel was all by shills. The oppressive torpor of that hour of an off-season, mid-week day deadened the atmosphere.

Then the live one, a brisk, compact man in a blue plaid shirt and tan sports jacket, came in through the alley entrance, went to the craps table and got directly into action. Ava Lowell, the croupier at the roulette wheel, a sad-eyed divorcee with a vague air of injury and reproach about her soft oval face, felt his vitality like an intrusion. She looked briefly across the casino at him, wondering for an unpleasant instant if she knew him, then decided she didn't.

Ava eased her weight from one leg to the other very slowly so as not to disturb the tired, pleasant heaviness of her body. She stood resting herself slackly against the edge of the betting layout table, her eyes remote, her fingers in languorous motion gathering and stacking the loose chips she'd raked in after the last mock play against the shill seated alone across from her.

The ball slotted and though there were no real players to hear she spoke the winning number aloud. To assure wins the shill had scattered her bets all over the layout. Ava raked in the losing bets quickly, measured out the wins more deliberately. Getting the losses rapidly out of sight and

5

lingering over the payoffs was house policy, the theory being to expose prospective players for a longer period to the sight of winning. There weren't any prospective players nearby. She set the ball spinning again, feeling like an automaton.

The man in the sports jacket was making a lot of noise at the craps table and her attention moved, will-less, toward him, a slight frown around her sad brown eyes. No; she didn't know him. It was just that he somehow reminded her of the dream she'd had last night . . . or rather yesterday afternoon, since she slept days.

Like all recent dreams, it had been horrible: She had been in a small shadowy room, alone and yet *not* alone. She looked in a mirror and saw that some of the shadows had gathered themselves into a dark mass. She tried to turn to look directly at it but it was visible only in the mirror. When she looked it was always motionless, but each time she looked it was a few inches closer to her back. It moved only in the split-second blinks of her eyes. Then it was at her lovely hair and she struck at it but it was bodiless. She tried to scream and was voiceless. Then the cloud was gone and she looked in the mirror and her head was shaved.

As she forced her attention back to the roulette wheel, Ava's fingers touched reassuringly at her thick, light brown, shoulder-length hair, secured by a plain barrette at each temple and bound loosely in back by a narrow green velvet band. Shy all her life, there was an unassertive feminine charm and grace in her manner and movement. Of medium height with a slim, unspectacular figure, she looked neat in the Fourleaf Club uniform of tailored gray slacks and short-sleeved white blouse featuring four-leaf-clover buttons and *"Ava"* embroidered in green on the breast pocket. But even after a year of it the uniform of a gambling casino seemed strange. She never put on those man pants without a twinge of shame as if they were a public badge of failure as a woman.

Occasionally she nodded, half-listening, as the shill, an elderly widow with insomnia resumed her story of adjusting to the loss of her husband. Because, as her husband Dave had used to say—approvingly—she was a listening woman, and because, as he had once said later—despairingly—she had an affinity for failures. All the nowhere-going, the dead-stop, the backward-going people in the world knew

6

her as one of their own. The widow spoke of resigning herself. They all finally did resign themselves and seemed proud, as if accepting the defeat of a second-best kind of life and lowering the flag to permanent half-mast were a triumph. She pitied them. Sometimes she envied them. For herself she had tried desperately but futilely to stop loving Dave, knowing she could not, but must, live without him.

Ava had not wanted to divorce Dave, and he had not asked for a divorce. But she had become a serious liability to him and she'd offered him his freedom. She didn't delude herself that her motive had been pure and selfless. If she had stayed he would have had to quit the company in which he had made such fine progress as a young executive or else he would have had to endure watching lesser men with better wives pass him by. Such an injury to his pride and frustration of his ambitions would gradually have embittered him. And whether or not he ever expressed it openly, he would know her as the source of his pain and failure, not a sweetness but a poison, and even the memory of the beautiful thing their love had been would be gone.

"Hey! Where are you going with those chips?"

Ava stared in dumb surprise at the man seated across from her. Her hand had been in the process of raking in a stack of about ten chips off the board. Her hand froze. Her glance flicked anxiously over to the craps table where this man should have been playing. . . . He wasn't at the craps table—he was here, across from her, staring at her with bulging, amber eyes and talking in an excited voice.

"Put 'em back. You're not supposed to take in a win bet. Put my chips back on twenty-five."

"Twenty-five?" Ava said tonelessly. She saw that the elderly widow who had been playing at her wheel was over at one of the blackjack tables.

"Sure. Twenty-five. I was on it. Put the chips back."

Ava looked at the wheel. The little white ball was riding in the "25" slot. She didn't remember the widow's leaving. She didn't remember this man's coming. She blinked, wet her lips and with a sense of helplessness put the chips back on the "25" square.

"I guess," she said uncertainly, "I was half asleep."

"Think nothing about it." He smiled, relaxing. "I didn't mean to get tough." He glanced to the left and to the right and said in an undertone, "Hope I didn't get you in trouble. But I kept playing and playing that number. Put my last ten chips on it. Naturally when it hit—"

She smiled. Naturally. I—I'm sorry."

She remembered neither his buying chips nor making any bets. The chips were orange-colored. On the rim of the wheel housing she saw a single orange chip resting on a silver dollar. The denomination of chips, except the five- and ten-dollar ones, was not marked. Usually the chips were worth a dime; if more, she kept track of the value by placing a coin with the chip. She *did* recall putting that chip on the silver dollar. A moment later she remembered another fragment. She had taken a fifty-dollar bill from him, inspected it briefly, then inserted it into the slot of the table bank. The rest remained blank. She frowned intently as she counted out and nervously recounted thirty-five ten-dollar chips. She pushed them across to him.

"Can you cash them?"

She shook her head. "Unless you want three hundred and fifty silver dollars. The cashier's right over there."

He got up, smiling. Ava shifted her eyes. "You want a ten-dollar chip for those?" She indicated the chips on "25."

He shook his head. "Let 'em ride. Bad luck not to replay your winning number."

Ava set the ball spinning and watched it, aware that he stood watching her instead of the ball. She could feel a slow flush crawling up her neck. The ball dropped into "10."

"Damn!" he said. "Right beside it. The very next slot . . . Oh, well, you're a damn good dealer. Here!" He reached across and put two ten-dollar chips on the green baize beside her hand.

"Thank you, but that isn't necessary at all."

"I want you to have it . . . Ava." He winked at her. "I'll be seeing you." He strolled over to the cashier's office.

She closed her eyes. It was later in the East. She could visualize Dave at breakfast and she concentrated her thoughts to him saying, *Dave . . . I'm scared. . . . Dave, I can't stand it, I'm losing my mind. Dave, I'm scared.*

The stranger's "I'll be seeing you" probably meant nothing, Ava knew. Nonetheless if she stayed in town as usual for a meal after the shift he *might* see her. She hurried out of the Fourleaf Club and away from the casino area to the parking lot across the tracks. She drove out into the residential area at normal speed but she had a sense of

8

racing. There was a harried look about her soft brown eyes and she repeatedly flicked glances at the rear-view mirror. There had been something cynical about his broad, coarse face and a bullying quality about his bulging, amber eyes and the "I'll be seeing you," accompanied by that knowing wink, might have been a sort of threat.

She stopped at the little grocery where she had an account, then drove on to her apartment, one of a dozen one-room units in a group of one-story, flat-roof, concrete-block buildings forming a quadrangle around a small court. She entered, chain-locked the door, set down the groceries, and, still in hat and coat, went to the front window. She stood tensely at the edge of the closed venetian blind, one eye gazing fixedly at the entrance to the court.

She stood as though entranced for a full two minutes, watching for him. It was fantastic to expect him. He had not been around to see her drive out of the parking lot, hadn't followed her in a car and couldn't know where she lived, but she stood gripped by fear and at the same time by an intense anger. She loathed the creature, her whole instinct was revolted by him. She shook her head and went quickly to the closet and hung up her hat and coat. She went back to the window, but only briefly, knowing he couldn't possibly be coming.

Get hold of your senses, she told herself. There was something suspicious about the overintensity of her reaction to the mere thought of the man. She stripped out of the casino uniform and hurried into a nice little pink house dress. In the process she caught herself automatically avoiding as much as possible the sight of her pale, bared flesh. She washed her hands and face carefully in the bathroom, came out and set the little dinette table prettily, then began the preparation of her meal.

The dread which that man roused *might* be disguised sexual desire. Her eyes lighted with brief hope as the idea flickered like heatless flame, then vanished. That part of her was dead, she knew, to her regret. She had tried to rouse it these past few months by dates with men of all types. She had a continuing interest and affection for several of them, but never any sexual desire. On occasion she had even taken the memory of Dave as lover into bed with her and tried to recreate his touch and sensation, but it was a barren, depressing experience. Only Dave's actual body could bring her body alive.

9

Food helped and she had developed a big appetite. But she couldn't seem to put on weight and she felt weak most of the time in spite of vitamin supplements and several tonics that she took regularly. Now, though it was near her bedtime, it was breakfast time and her meal consisted of breakfast foods. She had cooked oats with cream and sugar, a whole pan of biscuits lavishly buttered, scrambled eggs, sausages, fried potatoes and two glasses of milk. She sat properly and ate slowly, remembering all of her manners with the exception of a pleasant countenance, and there was no purpose in that when there was no one to cheer. Now and then a wave of loneliness would pass over her and she would stop chewing, her throat too full for swallowing, and just stare for several seconds.

When she was done she washed the dishes, tidied up the little place, converted the sofa into a bed and went in for her shower. She bound her hair, adjusted the spray and stepped into the stall, a towel protecting her upper back from the chill of the tile while the spray warmed her full stomach comfortably.

The warmth and friction of the water gradually put a flush on her skin and she looked down at the slick pinkness and remembered something horrible from her very young girlhood. She had been visiting a farm with her grandfather and had gone into a cornfield with some older boy cousins who caught a small rabbit. With a pocket knife they had cut the fur around the neck, then peeled the fur down clear off its hind legs, skinning it alive. They had put it down, a raw thing, slick and pink and in agony, and they had laughed at the poor creature and at her when she fell on the ground screaming and vomiting. . . .

She felt suddenly giddy. She shut her eyes and clutched the flesh of her upper abdomen, her nails digging. She had no sooner banished that memory than two others involving bullies came into her mind. She had been in the second or third grade in school and almost every day a big boy chased a smaller one and always caught him and always made him beg and cry. The smaller boy would start to run even before he was chased . . . and she herself, a rabbity little thing, had looked at a certain rough boy with such scared eyes that he chased her in the park and made her stand still and lift up her dress and show her pants. There had been no sex connected with it in her mind, just fright and shame, and a sense of helplessness.

10

She looked at her thin, naked body, so depleted that she hadn't menstruated for four months, and knew she was still weak and defenseless. The rough creature who had somehow hypnotized and paralyzed her senses back there in the casino and had stirred up these dark, unhappy memories was strong. He was stocky and there was vigor about him, a look of excessive and highly compressed physical energy, the whole of him saturated with unmistakable, ruthless maleness. He was like a powerful magnetic field and, whether by repulsion or disguised attraction, he exerted some sort of force on her. He was ugly and horrible and she didn't *want* to be under his influence. . . . She began to cry softly, the tears flowing down her cheeks. . . . *Dave . . . Dave . . . I'm your girl.*

Two

Ava's parents had married young and had lived in her grandfather's house while her father continued his schooling. Ava had been barely three when they crashed to death while speeding home from a weekend party in Detroit. It was decided by everyone in the family except Ava that her grandfather, a widower and retired judge, was too old to rear a little girl, so she had been taken into the family of an aunt. The strange home frightened her and a pair of older cousins pushed her around and subjected her to rough "teasing," and within a year she changed from a lively, happy, aggressively friendly little charmer to a sickly "cry-baby."

Her only happy memories of that period were of her grandfather's visits, but even these were surrounded by pain and anxiety. She would begin to brighten at the mere prospect of seeing him. As the moment of his arrival approached she would become dangerously overstimulated and would have to run repeatedly to the bathroom to keep from wetting herself. The possibility that he should ever see her dirty and shameful was terrifying. At the sight of his tall figure and gentle, beautiful, smiling face she would run to him and cling possessively throughout his visits. Too soon he must go and because he did not want her to cry and because she was afraid to let her cousins see her cry, she contained her misery, but she lived only for his next visit. Finally he reclaimed her and brought her safely and permanently back home.

When Ava met Dave McKettrick at the college in Cincinnati where she was a freshman, she was living with her grandfather, He was sick with age and missed her terribly if she was out at night and though she was eighteen, she'd never had a serious date. She spent her evenings studying, playing the piano for him, reading to him there in the big old house which had always been home to her. He was her whole world and she had no sense of confinement; she loved him and liked their quiet way of life.

From the time she was old enough to listen he had talked to her, trying through many a solemn and joyous hour to impart the best of his wisdom and goodness to her, his flower, his good girl. And it pleased her to know that she had become the sort of demure, soft-spoken young lady he so highly prized. "Blessed are the meek," he had used to say.

She had seemed prissy to most of her contemporaries at the college. But Dave was older—twenty-five. He had a degree in engineering and he had recently been selected by his company for executive training and he was at the college for a course as part of the training.

Dave had noticed her several times during the first week of the semester. As he told it, he had seen a dainty figure in skirt, blouse and unbuttoned sweater who moved with short, quick, legs-together steps and wore pink or blue or white bobby socks that matched the ribbon in her long, bright blond hair. He had liked the timidity and mood of embarrassment about her. She was sunburned and her thin, bare legs were pink and he had come to think of her as the pretty little virgin with the blushing legs. In the second week of the semester he approached her directly for a date and she had scurried away. Ava hadn't the slightest recollection of that first meeting and even when he told her about it after their marriage she couldn't quite believe it.

The Dave McKettrick she met through a mutual acquaintance in the middle of the fall term was of medium height, with a compact but sturdy physique, and the neat, chiseled Anglo-Saxon features of the adman's fantasy of the "typical" American youth. His firmly molded lips could break into a warm, handsome smile, but there was a glint of calculation in his dark eyes, and he seemed aware of the sales value of things like good grooming, correct dress and the smooth manners of a career boy on the make. Yet he seemed incapable of brashly thrusting himself at her without an introduction or of entertaining such a thought as "the pretty little virgin with the blushing legs." She had liked him at once and had gone to a stage play with him on Saturday afternoon and for a short drive Sunday afternoon. For weeks they had afternoon dates and occasional lunches together and walks around the campus, but it was a companionship, not a romance.

Ava Lowell never thought about marriage except as a someday-maybe thing because it would have meant abandoning her grandfather. She planned to teach music in the public schools and stay with him. He was old, but he always had been as long as she could remember and she didn't believe his predictions of his own death. Dave not only understood and praised her attitude but felt freed by it since he wasn't planning marriage either. Neither of them had any expectations beyond the simple pleasure of each other's company and talk. He, of course, did most of the talking, and she fell happily into the familiar role of responsive, sympathetic listener.

He came from a small Nebraska farm and was a "poor cousin" McKettrick. It had been a financial struggle to put him through engineering school and his branch of the family had felt unusual pride in his placing in the top tenth of his class. They considered his career an honor to them and Dave felt an obligation to succeed as though he were carrying a banner for them as well as himself. The company he worked for was an empire with twenty-four branches in the U.S. and Canada and a network of subsidiaries throughout half the world and he conveyed to her the importance of his selection as an executive trainee. Ava had been truly impressed and glad for him.

Then the tone of his talk had subtly changed. He began to confide his fears that the school he had attended lacked class, and that he was up against brilliant men from MIT and other really important schools. The intense technical focus of his schooling left gaps in his general knowledge and he was never quite sure of himself among some of the highly educated, sophisticated people who sometimes patronized him and maybe laughed behind his back.

13

He didn't know what to like in art or music and she helped him there. Her grandfather lectured him on literature and history and recommended basic reading, pleased that Dave had the mind and the inclination actually to learn. At the time he had needed all the things she could provide, and not the least of these was her continual assurances that he was intelligent, personable, and endowed with the highest skills and finest character and must, inevitably, succeed. He would drink in her words and nod gravely and believe everything she said as though hers were the final and only meaningful authority. For her part she came to feel a profound involvement and partisanship and an almost maternal tenderness toward him.

By the following May they had come to the point where they could not miss a day seeing each other. They usually met outside the library and she often had a chance to observe him the moment he first saw her. His dark face would light up with a grin and he would quicken his pace, his whole being alerted and transformed with pleasure. Seeing and feeling his reaction to the simple sight of her would fill Ava with such emotion that tears often came to her eyes and her breast seemed to burst.

She was not astonished one June morning to look in her mirror and see that she glowed and was no longer tepidly pretty but beautiful. She thought that truly he had entered in unto her in a spiritual sense and had given her this woman-virtue of beauty while the essence of her had nourished his man's strength. She loved him and she would be his mate forever.

They were married on her nineteenth birthday in September. Her grandfather had said with a morose sort of cheerfulness that he would be free, now that she was safe and well loved, to go to his rest in peace. But the old darling had decided that death was not for him and had perked up and headed out on a world cruise at the same time she and Dave had gone on their honeymoon.

She was frightened on the wedding night and Dave didn't press her. The second night he did press her, but when she cried he relented.

"I wouldn't hurt you," he kept assuring her, "you know I wouldn't hurt you, dearest. Don't be afraid, Ava . . . Baby, don't cry." He sat on the edge of the bed, soothing her in the dark, petting her and every few moments kissing her cheek. When she was calm he stood up between

14

the twin beds and lighted a cigarette. He stood there smoking and watching over her till he finished his cigarette. Then he dropped to his knees beside the bed and gazed at her. "Don't worry about it. Just close your eyes and go to sleep and tomorrow you'll feel better and we'll have a wonderful day. Everything's going to be all right because I love you."

"Dave, I love you, too, and I *will* be a good wife. I swear it. . . . I want to and I *will*, darling."

"Now, now, you're getting upset. Just don't think about it."

"I don't want to be such a disappointment to you, Dave; I'm so ashamed." Her face was filled with sudden pain— pain for him.

"Of what? Of being what you are? An innocent girl, nurtured as tenderly as a flower. That's the girl I loved and married and if anyone should feel ashamed it's me for not realizing how special you are, how precious. I've treated your love as if it were small change, something you could give lightly and casually to any stranger. . . . I'm almost a stranger and I've rushed you as if there's no tomorrow.

"I brought you here to make you happy and give you a wonderful time and instead of that I've made you afraid. Listen, Ava, from now on, you're not to worry, because everything is going to go at your pace. Then, when you're sure of me, of how deeply I love you—and *only* then—the thing you're afraid of will happen, and you'll find it's nothing to fear, but a wonderful experience. But for now, you're not to give it a thought. I won't press you at all."

When he got into the other twin bed she lay for the longest time staring miserably at the ceiling and listening to him toss. She turned on her right side and he lay on his left, facing her. A lamp table, higher than the beds, stood between them, its top and legs forming a sort of frame through which they could see each other. They lay, open-eyed, peering at one another. Then Dave laughed silently.

"I see you."

"I see you, too."

"Can't you sleep, pet?"

"I'm lonesome." Ava extended a slim bare arm over to him and touched his face. "I could sleep if you were here, holding me in your arms."

He began to kiss her hand.

"You've got sugar fingers. And the most graceful hands

15

and arms. And the most adorable shoulders and the most exquisite breasts. See what just your hand does to me? That's why it's impossible for me to get in bed with you."

"Couldn't you just sleep? Please?"

"If I come over there somebody's going to lose something. It'll probably be me, losing my mind. No, Ava. I can't lie beside the body of the woman I love more than anything in the world and not respond to her totally. The instant you're aware of that simple physical male response you'll get tense and scared again. Next thing you'll be crying and I won't go through that again tonight. I've had all the failure in that department I can take just now. Go to sleep." He turned on his other side.

After a moment Ava sat up and slipped out of bed. He sat up and started to rise from the opposite side when she came onto his bed. She caught him from around the back, and standing on her knees behind him, pressed her cheek against his.

"It's not your failure, Dave. It's mine. I know it, but please say you still love me, anyway."

His aggravation dissolved and he laughed at her. "Well, since you put it so appealingly and say please . . . I still love you." He turned and lay on his chest and drew her down so her upper body lay against his chest. He held her face in both hands and pulled it close and kissed her lips and then lifted it a few inches and grinned up at her while she gazed solemnly and lovingly into his eyes. "Want to hear a dirty joke?"

"No."

"I prescribe this one. Once upon a time there was an innocent farm girl who went off to college in the big city—"

"Are farm girls innocent?"

"Some are, some aren't."

"In Nebraska?"

"If you mean the girls around where I lived, yes, all of them, as far as I knew. So when this girl went off to college her mother told her—"

"Honestly? You never—well, made love to any other girl?"

"You're the very first girl in my life. So her mother said, 'When you get off there in the big city, you be careful; don't you let any of them there slickers—' "

"Did you ever want to make love to any other girl?"

"Never."

"There was never anybody before you that I ever wanted

to be kissed by." She kissed his lips slowly, withdrew and smiled. "It's awfully sweet of you to lie to me, Dave. I don't want to know a single thing about any of the girls that've been in love with you . . . except, were any of them my type?"

"No. Besides, you're not a type. There isn't anybody like you. So the mother warned her that if she let a man kiss her and get on top of her she'd be pregnant. Well, a few weeks later the parents came to college to visit the girl and the girl suddenly pointed to a boy and cried: 'Look, Ma . . . that boy's pregnant!'" He stopped and laughed. "Get it? She'd been on top of him. And the moral of this story, Ava, is that you may think of sex as a fight and of yourself as being beaten up. That makes you afraid of me as if I were an enemy. But you'd lose the fear if I were the downed one . . . the partner on the bottom."

She rolled away and buried her face in the pillow, giggling.

"You liked that joke, h'm?"

She rolled onto her back, laughing out loud. "Yes, but what I was laughing at was the other—the idea of me being on top. I wouldn't know *how* to do it to you. . . ." She became aware that he'd turned on his side, and she could feel the heat and pressure of him against her hip. She sobered. "I'll go back to my own bed."

"Stay here," he said. He rolled on his back. "Nothing's going to happen." There was a long silence between them.

"Dave. . ."

"What?"

"You made me realize something. I *do* think of it as a fight. I think I know why I'm that way. You see, when I was young and in grade school I wanted to be the cleanest and best little girl there ever was so that my granddaddy would be proud and wouldn't ever be sorry that he took me back home. . . . But some of the kids resented me for being a teacher's pet and getting good grades and being quiet and careful about my clothes and hair. Everything about me irritated certain kinds of boys— the loudest and roughest and untidiest. They'd push me and hit me when they got a chance and try to muss me up. Sometimes I went home dirty and blubbering and I'd have to sneak in and let the housekeeper pretty me up before letting Granddaddy see me.

"Well, later, when I was in high school, I had begun to

17

be a woman, technically, and it horrified me because . . . because—" she groped, and she knew from the sudden heat in her face that she must be blushing—"being a woman was a secret sickness and dirtiness. I had a sense of falseness in relation to Granddaddy, who couldn't imagine that I was anything but . . . well, ethereal and bodiless and lovely. I was aware that I had become a sexual object, and somehow or other I had the notion that he was totally innocent in such matters. I didn't want him to have to know the truth about *me*."

"You thought your grandfather who had sired five children of his own was innocent about human nature?"

"His other children are part of another life. I'm really his only one. That's how I always felt and so does he," she said. "He'd always say in answer to any criticism of my personality by my aunts or uncles that my difference from other people was not a lack, was not a mere reaction against the unhappy circumstances of losing my parents, but an added quality. It was this quality that his sort of upbringing had tried to preserve . . . something like a thin, lyrical passage on a violin which would have been drowned or crushed by the ordinary blare and blatancy of coarser creatures. I always thought of the rough grade-school boys as the kind of coarser elements he meant.

"In high school it was this very same type that seemed attracted to me. Only instead of crude pushing and hitting, they now whistled and leered and made filthy remarks and tried to kiss me and feel me. They'd follow in packs in the halls and in cars on the street and I felt it as hostility, though I knew it was sex. I couldn't understand why I should be the type to attract them. Other girls had crushes on these boys, and they were prettier and sexier than I ever was. But those boys just plagued me. To me they meant sex and ugliness and my lowest self and I was determined to be my highest self. I wouldn't even let myself have romantic crushes on movie stars.

"I guess what I really did was repress my natural sexual instinct, but what I thought I was doing was living up to the highest ideals. Then you came along and fell in love with the kind of girl I had tried to be, and I fell in love with you and I was sure I'd been right all my life, that it was—well, fated."

She paused for a moment, her manner breathless, her eyes liquid and shining and begging him for understanding.

18

"Dave, tomorow night, I'm going to be ready—ready to be your wife in every way. I promise, darling. Tomorrow night!"

She stopped on the threshold, her eyes widening in astonishment. There had been two vases of roses in the room and he had cut off the heads and stripped off the petals to form a red carpet to the bed. Dave stood in his fresh, pale blue pajamas—on this night of her promise, the tomorrow of her hopes and resolves—a wide, handsome smile on his face, watching for her reaction, which he obviously expected to be delight. She had to fumble prettily as if too deeply moved to articulate; she couldn't let him see she thought it was silly and that she was embarrassed for him.

"Now you know how I feel about you," he said, huskily. He knelt and briefly pressed his face to her gown at the knees, then his caressing hands were lifting her feet out of her foamy white slippers.

He got up and backed off, watching her with bright eyes, and she knew what was expected. She plucked delicately at her nightgown, lifting it above her ankles and stepped with dainty, conscious grace onto the rose petals. She walked barefoot to the bed and turned to see Dave watching her dreamily .

"Again. . . It's beautiful. I knew it would be. You're simply beautiful, Ava."

He was in a sort of transport as she began to walk again, but she was aware of the petals, cool and slippery, mashing under her feet, and of herself as ordinary, everyday flesh acting out a fantasy that she could not even believe was Dave's. Yet it was for her sake that he was trying to endow the occasion with magic and she felt sorry for him and loved him more than ever. She stopped a few feet away from him and looked at him tenderly.

But his smile had tensed, the soft, easy pleasure draining from it, and there was that unnatural brilliance to his eyes which made her own gaze shy away. He was feasting himself on her body and she felt nakedly exposed. Her shoulders were bare and the nipples of her conical young breasts showed tenderly pink through the lacework of her nightgown and the open lacework revealed her navel and the pale lower slope of her stomach.

She noticed his male aggression in the contour of his

19

thin pajamas and her heart quickened with panic and she told herself she mustn't react that way. Suddenly she wished she had the art and spirit to be irresistibly seductive so that he would rush her blindly, his senses and restraint banished. She shifted her feet, her slender toes wriggling as she tried to work up the nerve to do something. . . . Then she did it. She swayed her hips from side to side twice in a deliberately slinky motion and gave him a sultry look and tried to grin. She stopped abruptly, cold with embarrassment, knowing she had no allure and must look absurd to him.

But he took a long, swift step and seized her around the body and began to kiss her bare shoulders and throat and then he kissed her mouth hotly, and holding the kiss lifted her and lay her on the bed. When he turned off the light and began to kiss her and caress her body and murmur tendernesses into her ear, Ava lay rigid.

She kissed his face and put her arms up around him and stroked his back trying to convey her love, but her fingers were stiff and cold. He sat up abruptly.

"Goddamned if I'm going to beg."

He switched on the lamp and stared bleakly at her. She looked at him with wide, shocked eyes and put her hand on his and whispered: "I can't help it."

"You'll have to help it."

"I know. And I will. I will."

"Thanks!" His mouth was bitter. He lit a cigarette. "Big favor. You'll try not to be disgusted with me."

"It's not that. I love you. You know I love you, Dave."

"Love!" He got up. He paced out into the room. He came back, sat down angrily, glared at her. "Love!"

She blinked, her eyes filling, and turned her face. "I love you so much—" she caught her breath—"I love you so much I would die for you."

He was silent, then he pressed her hand. "I know," he said softly.

"It's just that *that* isn't love."

He leaned over and kissed her neck. "Ah, now, baby, that's not true. You know that isn't true."

She turned and caught his face in her hands and kissed him ravenously. "You'll have to do it all. . . . I just can't think intelligently about it. . . . I just can't make myself believe it's got anything to do with love no matter how much I try. You do it—all of it!"

20

He mashed out his cigarette carefully, frowning at it, and then stood up. She lay on her side with her knees drawn up almost to her chest, her nightgown sheathing her legs, and stared widely at him, her eyes rolling up into the corners. He began to unbutton his pajamas, staring down at her in silence.

When he flung off the pajama top, showing the dark triangular mat of hair that covered most of his chest and upper abdomen, she wanted to giggle, but his mouth was straight and humorless. His hands went to the waistband of his pants and she expelled her breath, drew her legs up tighter and turned her face, burying it in the pillow. For long moments, he said nothing, did nothing. Then his hand burrowed between her face and the pillow and forced her to turn her head. She kept her eyes shut.

"Open your eyes," he said, tonelessly. "It's a man you married and it's time you faced it."

The command in his voice sent a shiver through Ava's body and her toes curled and she pulled her legs so tight against her body that her round little heels embedded in her upper thighs. Obediently she widened her eyes and stared, trying not to see but seeing that he was stark naked and fiercely passionate. Her senses swam. She thought she would faint. She covered her face.

"Oh . . . oh . . . it's terrible, it's worse than I imagined," she whispered. "You'll hurt me. . . . Please don't"

He was pulling her hands from her face and jerking her up into a sitting position, then a standing position. He lifted her nightgown to her waist and when she tried to catch it he said, "Stop it," and she obeyed and he pulled it off over her head. She stood tremblingly naked, feeling weak and tiny against him, her hands moving automatically to protect her intimacy, but he had turned to the bed and was arranging two pillows atop each other in the middle of it.

"Get on the bed. Lie with the pillows under your hips."

"Dave . . . Dave . . . I feel giddy; I think I'll faint. I think I'm sick. . . ."

"Did you hear me? Do I have to put you there myself?"

"No," she replied meekly.

She arranged herself as ordered. She lay with her midsection arched upward and crossed her ankles, holding her legs tight together. Then he was looking down at her and grinning and her face flamed and she covered her eyes

21

with her forearm. She heard the snick of the lamp and knew the room was dark and she could feel the sag of the bed as he came onto it.

Then his hands were embedded in the soft flesh of her hips and he was shifting her position as if her body were a machine and she choked back a soft cry of despair, feeling utterly humiliated. Then he was pulling, gently at first, then angrily, at her crossed ankles. She tried to roll on one side, but he flattened her roughly and held her motionless. Then he was between her knees, his lower body coming closer and closer. His hands, holding her like a vise, were hurting her, until finally his heat and maleness were in contact with her body. He paused, and for just an instant he was Dave again as he whispered gently, "It's going to hurt, dearest . . . but I love you. . . ."

Ava held her breath, tense and quivering all over. Then it came, a hard thrust that tore her virgin flesh and drove brutally onward, ripping at her insides with a sensation like raw flame. She bit her forearm to keep from screaming and tried to drag herself to the head of the bed but his body impaled her. She braced her feet and lurched upward and twisted against him but she was mashed and held securely.

The hot feel of her own blood trickling over her upper thighs and buttocks made her desperate. She gasped: "Stop," but he continued agonizingly, as if he no longer cared about her feelings.

She lay supine, helplessly submitting to the punishment, her arms and legs inertly unprotesting, her eyes scalding with tears, her throat choked with useless crying. His body was caught up in a steady, ruthless frenzy, and when she thought it couldn't possibly go on any longer, the tempo of his violent motion increased and shook her body like a rag doll. He became utterly wild. His penetration stabbed relentlessly deep and a shuddering spasm went through him and she thought something had ruptured within her. Then he freed her and presently he was petting her and trying to stop her crying. But she was almost convulsive, feeling used and beaten and hopelessly degraded and it was hours before she got herself calm and back in perspective.

For a long time afterward Ava had continued to feel an indignity and defeat about the sexual act and her only pleasure had been derived from the knowledge that Dave enjoyed it. Then gradually she overcame her sense of aversion and experienced the purely sensual gratifications. But she felt and continued to feel that the sensual pleasure was dependent on her deeper unity with him, and that no other man could ever rouse her sexually.

Three

From the honeymoon they went to Dave's new assignment in Houston; a year later it was Wheeling, West Virginia; then Seattle, Washington; next a year in Rochester, New York. Like other young executives being groomed for important positions, the experience gave him a comprehensive grasp of company operations, and each time he moved on, he moved up. He never knew where he might go next, and worse, he might not be transferred at all, but stay, judged to have reached his ceiling. Whether or not it was calculated, these annual uprootings, by discouraging ties to place or people and making a man's sense of solidity and achievement dependent on the company, focused his strongest loyalties on the organization.

In each new place a furnished house always awaited them, along with a ready-made pattern of social life and friends within the tight little community of company men and wives. Everybody was always co-operative, friendly and helpful right down to the point of trying to tell Ava where to shop and have her hair done. It was expected that everyone like everyone equally and immediately as though total strangers were old friends, which she considered false. Dave made friends quickly and easily in each new environment and he seemed to adapt at once, but actually each transfer upset and for weeks he felt "no place" except with her.

It soothed him to come home to her, to eat her wonderful meals, many of them featuring recipes she had conscientiously learned from his mother, to talk to her in the night, to "unjangle himself." Sometimes he would flop on the bed and say: "Sugar Fingers, my eyes are glassy and my cheeks are sour from fake smiling," and she would stroke his cheeks and eyelids and he would chuckle like a baby and wrap her in his arms. She gloried in her role as his solace and joy.

Ava's relationship with most of the other wives was at best a truce, because they traveled in packs. They were eternally socializing, gathering at each other's houses or the club pool or the beauty parlor to fritter away time, gabbing about clothes, gossiping, discussing intimate details of marital life. Ava gave out no bedroom tidbits about Dave and herself and she was determined not to abandon such disapproved activities as reading and serious music. Consequently she was never a member in good standing of "the gang." Dave applauded her; he wanted her to retain her identity.

When one other person or couple was involved she was warm and flowing, either as hostess or guest, but large groups gave her stage fright. At the parties including men as well as their wives, she felt self-conscious and heavy, neither glib nor witty nor good at games. At those first parties she had focused on Dave, watching and listening to him adoringly. This had pleased him privately but embarrassed him publicly. She became less obvious about the fact that he was the center of her world, but evidently he wasn't so overjoyed with her success. One night he came home from a party in a temper with her.

"So the honeymoon's over. You're just one of the girls."

"What are you mad about?"

"Didn't take you long to learn to spread yourself thin. I looked at you a couple of times tonight and except for the color of your hair I'd have sworn you were Sal Jenison. Have you been palling around with her?"

"I certainly have not."

"You act like it. You don't have to promote yourself with me any more. But Joe Baggley, he's a thousand a year more than I am, and so's Cam Fredericks—so *their* jokes, somehow, suddenly, have *flavor*. If you could have heard yourself tinkling with laughter and seen yourself being so *charmed*."

She had begun to grin at him. "You really love me."

He snorted. "*You* think it's jealousy. It's nothing of the kind. I refuse to see you turn into a creature like that Sal Jennison. I can dance with that girl with my eyes closed and tell you exactly what a man's salary is this year and what it's likely to be seven years from now simply by the amount of coo she puts into her greeting to him. She uses

24

her personality like a precision instrument. If you're planning to turn into—" The absurdity of the accusation made him stop and grin suddenly. He mussed her hair and kissed her.

She laughed up at him and teased: "Darling, you *were* jealous."

"I was *sick* with it."

Her happiness and the success of her marriage were clear to her grandfather. She kept in regular touch by letter and on special days by phone. He visited them a few days in Houston and next summer they were with him in Cincinnati for a week of Dave's vacation. He was as ageless and alert as ever, and when he came, that second winter, to spend Christmas with them in Wheeling, Ava could scarcely believe the changes she saw. The last few months had taken a frightening toll; she knew it couldn't be an alienation which made her see him more objectively. He had become wispy and palsied and the age lines had deepened and masked him, and sometimes his eyes went vague and his thoughts lapsed in mid-sentence, and at other times he became shrill with false buoyancy and talked incoherently of things in his childhood and once he even called her by another name.

Most distressing of all was when he would pull himself together and see his own deterioration. "I thought," he said on one occasion, "I'd have more sense than to keep hanging on till I became a sickening caricature of myself. How I wish I could have spared you this, Ava! I shouldn't have come. I thought if I saw *you*, that the will and strength would be in me again. But, accept it, child, resign yourself, sing no sad songs for me. . . . There's no reversing the tide. . . ."

He broke her heart. Two months later pneumonia took him and he was gone before she reached him.

Oddly, Dave was gloomier than she was after the funeral. She didn't cry and it worried him, and she had to explain.

"But I'm not internalizing it, Granddaddy told me time and time again to accept it. He didn't want to go on when he knew it would be deterioration and worse pain every day. The one thing he did have to be happy about was my marriage. He knew it had to be this way, that you're my life; we're the living and the future. I've known that for a long time. Where you are is where I belong. . . . You're

25

my center. I try to make myself yours. I'm your woman, your home; that's all I want to be. . . ."

Dave's small-town upbringing had carried with it a simple code, not unlike her own, of honest and direct relationships with people, but he considered his career a jungle in which all the rules he knew were reversed. Among his fellow workers, superiors and subordinates the fight for advancement was continual but hidden. Direct expression of hostility was barred; everyone operated under a cloak of good will, there were no frowns; therefore the public, professional smile had a hundred subtle shadings and meanings—few of them were honest expressions of liking. Everything had a political angle and he preferred, as did Ava, that their social life be personal and based on true friendship, and though it was impossible to take the office politics entirely out of sociability he didn't want her involved and compromised.

Particularly after her grandfather's death Dave liked to think of himself rather heroically in relation to her. He was not only her sole protector but, as he said in his confident, playful moods when he was enjoying her alone, he was a modern caveman who carried his club out into the dangerous world and came home with the plunder for the delectation of his mate. Her place was in the safe cave, her role to heal and love him and strengthen him for the next day's bout.

He had wanted her to be just the sort of person she was—that had been her very meaning to him. He hadn't wanted her to change, and she hadn't. But circumstances, after the move to Chicago, had changed, and so had her meaning to Dave.

The promotion and transfer to the heart of empire were special. Dave had reached a plateau along with the very best of the young executives. Some among them were destined for top-echelon positions and while the concealed competition among them was stronger, so was Dave's confidence. He was selected to accompany various top-management men on important trips for divisional meetings and conferences in different parts of the country and then he was entrusted with several trips on his own. He became more certain that he was going to get an assistant-branch-plant managership within a year. He'd pace and talk, aglow with their future, pointing out that from assistant it was an easy step to plant managership, and success there led to a divisional vice-presidency.

He was gone a lot, two or three weeks out of some months, and she missed him fearfully. After Dave became conditioned to jet flights and living in the best hotels on a good expense account and meeting casually with the highest echelons of the company, home must have seemed dull, trivial. Ava sometimes felt their reunions weren't as sweet for him as for her.

He began to achieve the polish he'd always feared he lacked and she began to worry that he was developing while she stood still. He laughed at her fears and assured her that his success was *their* success, but she sensed a growing reserve about him.

Once he said that her trouble at parties was that she sought her own kind and tended to huddle with other self-conscious people and she should try to cultivate other types—he didn't quite say, cultivate "people who counted," but that was the implication. Sal Jennison, the "horrible example" of a wife that Dave had detested that first year, had reappeared on the scene. She and her husband had arrived in the Chicago main office by another route at the same time as Dave. One night at a small club dance Dave made the same remark about Sal using her personality as a precision instrument, which automatically calculated a man's importance in the company—but this time Dave said it laughingly, almost admiringly. Yet, on the whole, there was no alienation between them.

Ava would never forget, however, the height and sudden depth of Dave's mood when he came home to their roomy Chicago flat one Thursday afternoon an hour or so early. He was carrying three gift packages and she sensed and fell in at once with his mood. He kissed her lengthily, then gave a spank because his drink wasn't ready and she uttered a loud and piteous cry and hustled off, giggly with excitement. When she returned with his cocktail the three gifts were on the piano bench which he had set in front of the davenport. She slipped off her shoes and sat little-girlishly cross-legged on the center cushion and began to unwrap her gifts—a book, a record, some piano music—while he wandered about the room sipping the drink and enjoying her pleasure.

He loved pampering her and she adored his impulse to do it. But the very paternalism of him on such occasions, instead of making her feel small and lovable, gave her a feeling of grossness and imposture, as though she were a poor substitute for the real child that his and her own instincts craved. This feeling would begin as painful twinges within her breasts, but presently the sensation would radiate and descend in continuous chains of hot flashes through her belly that settled and built up in a mounting fever in her private parts. She would feel an animal cunning that shamed her as she wondered how she could ever trick him into impregnating her. He didn't feel ready for kids, and although there was no doubt in her mind that his will should dominate and she hadn't the strength nor desire to oppose him further in words, she dreamed of and experimented with seduction.

She'd lost all sexual shame with him and didn't hesitate to take the aggressive role. She remained physically desirable to him and she could bring him to passion against his original mood, but his control never failed to the point of forgetting protection. Whenever he sensed she'd been trying to rush him off guard he deliberately prolonged the session, remaining virile and in command of her and of himself for what seemed hours, bringing her to ecstasy time and again and taking high pleasure in exhausting and mastering and in a sense punishing her.

Sometimes she would lie awake and think about those sessions and she'd become roused and begin to stimulate him to desire while he slept. He'd wake fierce and hot and she'd be sure she had succeeded. But always he took precautions before coming to her and making her forget any intention she might have had beyond the immediate and exquisite pleasure of him.

He had an endearing formula for presenting her with gifts. The physical ones were only build-ups, then he would come to the "ice cream at the bottom of the soda," which was a piece of good news. The good news this time was that he was one of twenty-four young executives invited with their wives to a party, two weeks from Saturday, at the home of none other than R. K. Clements, a ranking VP and member of the board of directors. The others invited were a highly select group, and Dave's inclusion among these star performers was tantamount to a double-jump promotion at the least.

As he explained the significance of the invitation which she would be getting in the next day's mail he moved about the room with a sort of gliding strut. He soared, his words and easy laughter flowed, breaking only to allow her to add her exclamation points of approval. He basked in his own satisfaction and her admiration. His conceit was manly and exciting and his enthusiastic confidence carried them both strongly. His celebration went on in the front room for twenty-seven minutes—she knew exactly because she had something in the oven—and for another twenty minutes in the kitchen and dining room. Then, starting on his salad he looked like a man who has been strolling with his eyes on the stars and abruptly steps off the roof. He looked across at her with such a dismal look of deflation that she cried out in protest.

"I know what you're thinking—that I'll be a stick and embarrass you. Dave, don't *you* lose confidence, or I'll be licked before I start."

"*Me* lose confidence? That's absurd," he said hastily. "I've told you a million times what you are and what you've got—warmth and natural affection and a fine mind; and you're pretty and you've got a charming figure. You've got it all over any of them. Plus, you know I'm proud of you, that I'll be there, that nobody's going to hurt you. If only you could keep these things uppermost in your mind and just clamp down on your vague, childish fears!"

"I can. I've got two weeks to prepare and I'll be ready. I'll just keep in mind that your ability and success are the reason we'll be there. That way I won't feel that too much is expected of me so I won't fear failure, won't feel inadequate. Don't worry," she laughed, "I'll sparkle plenty!"

The Saturday night of the party, her hair and ornaments and lipstick and gown and fingernail and toenail and shoes and fur wrap, in fact everything but Ava herself, did sparkle plenty. But her breathing was shallow, her eyes glittery and jumpy, her cold fingers nervous. She went out into the living room where Dave, utterly suave in his new evening jacket, was waiting. She posed, managing to fetch up a small, uncertain smile.

"Lovely," Dave said. He clapped his hands in silent applause and smiled automatically. The immediacy of his response sent a vague chill through her. She knew he hadn't really formed an opinion yet. Behind the smile as he came toward her, his eyes inspected her apprehensively. It was as if he weren't Dave, her husband, expressing a private feeling about his wife, but Dave the Corporation's man being agreeable, and alert to put himself on record with the correct attitude. As he strolled, drink in hand, in a circle around her, she understood that he was judging her with his public, career-conscious eye.

The skirt of her ankle-length, pink satin strapless gown was full, the bodice tight around her graceful, narrow waist. Her fair skin was so delicate that here and there the blue tracery of a vein showed charmingly on the pale nakedness of her frail shoulders and the upper roundings of her soft breasts. Tiny pearl clusters ornamented her neat pink ears and a silver and bead chain was laced through her bright hair, which was upswept, exposing the loveliness of her neck.

The hair stylist had assured her that the formality of the upswept hairdo had a poise and regality about it. But if it was at all regal on her it was at the child-princess level; she had no queenly hauteur or will to command. As Dave inspected her she thought hopelessly that her vulnerability and passivity and general air of retreat no longer appealed to him, that he was now looking for "woman-in-charge" qualities. Though he paused in back of her and kissed her shoulder, his lips chilly from his drink, and then came around and sniffed appreciatively at her perfumed breasts and kissed them too, there was something mechanical about it and he slyly took one of her hands, feeling her fingertips to gauge her inner mood.

"Your fingers are cold," he said accusingly, though he smiled. "I'll get you some wine." He walked across the room and she knew from the unswinging set of his shoulders that he was aggravated.

She almost spilled the wine, increasing his annoyance and her own sense of inadequacy. For blocks in the car he sat in a tight, accusing silence until she cried out thinly: "I know you want to yell at me. Well, *do!*"

"You *let* yourself freeze up."

"That's not *fair!*"

"You think, and I've encouraged you to think, you're that princess who was so tender a rose petal bruised her." He snorted derisively. "You're not so precious you can't give out a little. You think I don't have to? You think I don't have to compromise myself in my job? Why should *you* be immune? Why should I do it all? Where do you exist anyway, Ava? On a cloud far from the madding crowd? It's nice up there, but get the hell down, baby. Real fast. That's an order!

"You're going into that party swinging and slugging the

30

same as me. If a little faking is going to sully your precious soul that's just too tough. I'm sick and tired of living down here in the dirt and being looked on from above with moral contempt by my own wife as if you're so damned superior. . . . And don't you dare cry!"

"Cry? You make me so mad. You're being so outrageously unjust and accusing me of things you know are lies. . . . I'll go in there sluggging, don't you worry." She moved angrily away from him and sat quiveringly in her corner of the seat. He glanced over at her scowlingly. The scowl gave way to a grin.

"Don't try to make up with me," she snapped

He laughed aloud, jabbed his forefinger at the seat beside him. "You come right over here and sit where you belong."

After a few minutes she moved back beside him. He slipped an arm around her shoulder and hugged her.

"You're a real spitting little cat when you want to be," he chuckled. "You know I didn't mean all that crap."

"Well, whether you did or not, it worked. I'm so hot and bothered that I'm not self-conscious at all. I'm going to make it at that party!"

He walked her in so proudly and possessively that she felt invulnerable. She got through the initial introductions with flying colors. Everyone smiled on her and with her and she seemed set. . . . Then it began, the slow seepage of her confidence, a tiny chill of uncertainty replacing her warmth. She began to sense the reality of competitiveness in the faces of the other wives, the cagey circling and positioning taking place among the men under the cover of amiability, and she found herself retreating out of the edge of things, into the shadows, feeling alone and unreal and lost. When Dave saw it and flashed her a private tight-mouthed warning, her toes curled and she tried to ease back into the swing of things, to make herself noticed. She couldn't.

Dave knew she had tried. He knew she'd achieved at least a brief success, and when they got home that night he was not angry with her but sorry and he tried to be understanding. They talked till dawn, and their hopes about her came alive again.

But over the next three months at a dozen formal and informal gatherings she made it hopelessly clear that her best was not enough.

And then it happened. Dave's double promotion didn't

come through. In fact, for the first time, he got no promotion at all.

And the reason for it was made clear to Ava by the wife of Dave's immediate superior. Ava was the reason. If Dave was ever to be given a branch-plant managership where he would be the company's representative and an important civic figure, he would have to function socially. And social functioning was chiefly the department of the wife. She had been judged and found lacking. She recalled that a number of women higher in the hierarchy had paid unexpected calls on her, and these calls had actually been tests.

The woman who told her about it was sympathetic. Ava should have been interviewed by management early in her marriage . . . or preferably during her engagement.

"You mean if Dave had only known *before* marriage," Ava remembered saying to the woman, "he'd have realized I wasn't the sort of wife the corporation needed."

"Now, Ava, you mustn't be bitter."

"*Bitter?*" she'd cried. "Bitter? I'm—I'm desperate!"

"It isn't hopeless, not at all hopeless. This need only be a temporary setback. I'll make an appointment for you with the chief of personnel."

She had had many appointments. Batteries of psychological tests, which she must have failed miserably. The personnel man did his best, though, advising her in detail how she could go about becoming someone else. She had tried to become what Dave needed. But she became obviously artificial; worse, not better. Then she tried liquor and became disgusting. Dave would smile at her, not with his private smile, but with his glassy-eyed public smile, and tell her it didn't matter. He told her to forget it, that she was *his* wife, not the company's. The subject was not mentioned again.

They began pretending that all was as before. She knew, however, that he was putting out feelers with other companies in the same industry. But his bargaining position as a passed-over executive wasn't good, and he'd have had to take a step down, with no guarantee in a new company that his wife wouldn't be a handicap there, too.

She couldn't stand going on that way. The thing was festering like poison in him and demoralizing him badly; there was no estimating what his loyalty to her might be costing him in every sense.

To know what his love for her was doing to him and that

she and her love for him were his enemy, was torture. She wished herself dead, and fought against the growing awareness of the only possible solution. She couldn't escape it. In the middle of one summer night, when Dave was out of town and she was aching with loneliness for him, she began to cry softly in her bed, realizing and accepting what she must do.

She began a game called "I want a divorce," which they played for weeks. It was a complex, tricky and new game, but they both understood the main rules. Unstated Rule Number One said: "If either party refers to the real problem, the game ends." An equally important rule forbade mentioning that a divorce would benefit Dave. Another rule was that each must give the other tips on their next moves.

Thus, when Dave said her words were inconsistent with her loving actions she began to show total indifference to his departures and returns from trips; to fail to get up and make his breakfasts; to give him slapdash dinners or none; to let him come home to an empty house several evenings; to barely endure his love-making.

Finally he said: "You really *don't* love me any more."

"I've said it and said it. Why do you want to hold a woman against her will? I thought you had more pride. I want to live my own life, move back to Cincinnati. Take up where I left off when I got infatuated with you."

"Infatuated! I haven't heard that word since Queen Victoria." He exploded with laughter. "You know the trouble with you, Ava? You don't live in this century; you're archaic, an anachronism—the perfect copy of your grandfather with all his artificial standards and fake niceties."

"You never spoke to him that way to his face when he was alive!"

"Certainly not. He was a charming old gentleman; I appreciated him as I do any fine specimen in a museum. He was quaint and sweet, the way *you* were—and—well, the way you still are."

It cut her and tears sprang to her eyes and she forgot the rules and cried out: "I know what I am. It's been pointed out to me all my life—and nobody liked me for being a quaint, sweet, meek, little thing. But *he* did and he loved me and I didn't care what *they* thought. I never knew *you'd* join them!"

"Don't cry, baby. . . . Ah, sweetheart, you know I love

you. . . ." Crying, she twisted free of his arms and ran to the bedroom.

He followed at once and she shrilled at him: "Oh, blessed are the meek. . . . Oh, blessed are the meek. You know what I say? DAMNED are the meek!"

"You're hysterical, baby."

"Yes. Out of my mind. And thank *God,* because I *hate* my mind. And my whole life, and you and everything. If you don't sign the papers and let me go to Reno I'll—I'll—drink and make a fool of you and I'll go with men, with men you work with, and I'll slut around and make you hate me. . . ."

Ava had kept it up, relentlessly, and in the end Dave had consented and she had come to Reno and established residence at a desert "hen ranch" for women taking the "cure."

There had been a curious feeling about those six weeks as though she were gradually slowing and cooling. She knew she had been hysterical, and Dave knew. She went to bed each night, quick with the hope that she'd be miraculously awakened by his long-distance phone call or his actual presence; each morning she would awaken in that strange, empty land with the knowledge leaden in her stomach that her god had not reclaimed her. To wipe out the unendurable endlessness of idle time she had wandered around the casinos staring at the games and players with an inner shudder of pity and fear, feeling that this was a world of lost creatures. She would no more have indulged in gambling than . . . than she'd have stripped naked in public and rolled in slime.

She didn't know why she accepted a job as shill, except that she had been approached by one of the casino managers and to have refused would have required more effort than to accept. When her divorce was granted, her sense of slowing and cooling became something closer to motionlessness. She had not one real plan for the future—somehow she never expected the future to arrive.

Then the Fourleaf Club offered to train her and take her on as a dealer. She accepted for a confusion of reasons. A job requiring her to meet hundreds of new people was a form of punishment which at the same time might cure her meekness and perhaps make her the successful extrovert sort of woman Dave didn't really want but needed, and then she could go back to him. If that didn't work, this

34

climate of strangeness would be a perfect escape from the despair and failure in another world. But the fundamental reason she took the job was that it was something rather than nothing and she took it from sheer inertia.

She held the job through inertia, too, this time on the part of management. She wasn't very good at her job. As a blackjack dealer she still shuffled amateurishy, partly, she knew, because of her grandfather's belief that only "hard" females were deft with cards. She lacked the alertness necessary to the tempo of the ruffian game of dice at the craps table. Even at the roulette wheel she flustered under the stress of peak-hour crowds and heavy play.

Just taking such a job had had the odor of abandoning herself to corruption but the management felt protective toward her and indulged her ineptness because, ironically, she was such a nice girl.

Four

Ava had used to be a happy waker, but today as usual she woke near dusk with the usual dull headache. She lifted an edge of her sleep mask, looked at the clock and dropped back listlessly. She had had an endless dream of floating bodiless over a bleak landscape of twisted black rock, dull brown cinders and gray ash which was Hell—not a fire-and-torture world at all, but a burned-out lifelessness.

There was nausea in her stomach and a secretion of bitter fluid at the base of her tongue. She began to swallow rapidly. Then a rhythmic series of small convulsions rippled along the muscles of her abdomen, increasing in tempo. She clenched her teeth and exerted her whole will but it was useless. She tore off the sleep mask, flung out of bed, raced to the bathroom and vomited.

Afterward she sucked in and spat out several mouthfuls of clean water. She used a mouth wash, then soap and water on her face and hands, feeling loathsome. She went back and sank exhaustedly on the bed, her head throbbing, a raw trembly feeling in her whole body. She lay on her side in a long blue flannelette nightgown, chilly but too sick to pull the covers over her. A cramp hit her lower stomach and she pressed her hand against it, noticing that it was bloated. She drew her legs up against her stomach, then just lay as completely motionless as possible. She half-dozed, then another cramp in her stomach roused her. She stared sightlessly toward the kitchen area, kneading her fingers cautiously into the flesh of her lower stomach. Not exactly a cramp . . . there it was again. . . .

She sat up and lifted her nightgown to the navel and stared down at herself. There was a definite rounding like a half-melon under the skin.

She dropped the nightgown and began to laugh humorlessly. In spite of these pregnancy-like sicknesses she'd been having and in spite of having been "a pretty little virgin with blushing legs," it wasn't likely she'd have a virgin birth.

She got into slippers and robe, went over to the tiny refrigerator and drank a glass of cold tomato juice. She freshened herself in the bathroom, brushed her hair and put on a knit dress. Opening windows to air out, she put on a hooded ski-style coat and galoshes, wanting to flee from this stagnant place.

There was a slow snowfall illuminated by the lights from the other apartments around the court when she went out on the stoop. She glanced at her empty mailbox, tossed her newspaper into the apartment and hurried out of the court to her garage.

She headed away from town and drove along, the wipers swinging hypnotically, with no particular destination in mind. There was little traffic, a ranch truck, an old jalopy or two. The snow veil obscured the lights of the ranches dotted in the distance. The edges of the road were not well defined, neither ditched nor shouldered, and she decided to slow down and drive off into the desert. The ground was bumpier than it looked and she drove at a crawl. After a quarter of a mile she stopped completely.

She shut off the lights, the engine idling, her mind idling with the question of how they managed to lead the exhaust fumes into a car. The diameter of a garden hose was smaller than the exhaust pipe. . . . Well, adhesive tape, wide adhesive . . . but for the hose to enter the car a window would have to be left open—but the opening could be stuffed with rags.

Switching off the engine, she got out of the car and began to walk slowly, watching her footing. She thought of snow as refreshing and lovely, but it kept gathering on her eyebrows and lashes and dissolving wetly just inside the tops of her galoshes and a cold breath from the ground chilled her bare thighs and the tomato juice seemed to slosh, cold and unassimilated in her stomach.

One afternoon as a young girl she had been walking in the park with her grandfather. For some reason they were unhappy with one another and they trudged along, solemn and silent. He looked down and saw her catching snow-flakes on her tongue and knew her spirits were up and his own gloom dissolved. They began to smile at each other slowly and lovingly. The cherished memory of that moment twinged in her breast. She stuck out her tongue for a moment, then withdrew it, thinking that the sweet foolishness of a child was the sour silliness of a grown woman.

She came to a stop, so weary that she thought she would just sink down and let the snow settle over her and numb her into drowsiness and sweet, dreamless sleep. Turning slowly around, full circle, she stared into the blur of snow which concealed the towns and houses, the towering Sierras somewhere to the west, and the sky itself.

The partially snow-covered desert growths were stunted and gnarled and twisted and spiny and needled and tough and ugly, but awesomely beautiful when you knew, as she knew, that these shapes and ugliness were the will to live against hopeless odds. She tried to shame herself for her cowardly submission to death. Go back, go back. . . . She took a few steps toward the dark outline of her car. She stopped again. To *what?*

Her grandfather had used her occasional childhood sicknesses to educate her about the vastly complex, miraculous functioning of the body, and recovery had always given her a sense of pride in her body. As he had said, it didn't know how to surrender. It fought its enemies relentlessly till they were routed. He would show her how the tiniest cut or bruise called battle forces and repair troops into immediate and ceaseless action. There was an instinctive joy in the flesh and it did not know how to die. A person could lose arms and legs and half his flesh and still *it would not know how to die.* The sight of her in the mornings, refreshed with healing sleep and cleanly glowing with good health would lift him with joy. But now the time had come when there was only sickness, day after day after empty day.

She moved her feet up and down, resisting the cold, and shook her head at a sudden realization. Last night . . . last night in the casino she had had a period of amnesia. Her breathing came almost to a stop and she shook her head slightly and stared out at the nothingness, resisting the sudden inner brilliance and lucidity. . . . Resistance was useless. She remembered everything.

She took off one glove and skimmed off some clean top snow. She rubbed it against her cheeks till they stung pleasantly.

He had liked her. That coarse creature had liked her and he'd asked for her address. And she had told him!

More than that. She had paid him off on the number "25" when his bet had actually been on "24!"

She had let him bluff her. Her will and her mind had submitted to the dominance of his cheating, criminal mind.

Ava walked back to her car and got in with an odd, numbed sort of resignation. He was coming to her apartment at seven-thirty.

Her own mind was her enemy—was death.

Whatever his mind was, whatever he was, death was worse. She started the car and circled back to the road, heading for home and her first date with the creature. For a few more minutes she refused to credit him with a name or to admit she remembered it. Then she shrugged and smiled wryly. Tom was his name.

There was a riddle, Ava thought when she re-entered her apartment a few minutes before seven-thirty. In the remote landscape of the unfamiliar desert, where the snow had obscured the outer reality, she had felt an inner clarity of mind; now, where all was too distinct and familiar, she felt an inner confusion. She might easily have misunderstood whatever had been said or done by Tom back there in the casino, considering the state she had been in . . . and might still be in. She shook her head, faint anxiety shadowing her eyes as she stood at the closet hanging up her coat. She went over and reconverted the bed into a sofa, closed the windows and switched on the heater, moving, in spite of a sense of rushing, with deliberation as if to demonstrate to herself that she was in control.

When the bell rang she went over and opened the peephole. There stood Tom, bulky in a snow-flecked hat and coat. She paused to draw a long deep breath, then opened the door.

"Hello, Ava."

Her heart was in her throat. She nodded, unable to speak and moved back along the arc of the opening door as he stepped up and in. His glance, briefly wary, swept the whole apartment. Ava shut the door, a tingling numbness in her fingers. They stood a yard apart looking at one another in complete silence, and she could feel the mood of furtiveness, the breath-suspended sense of conspiracy between them.

His bulging, amber eyes were bright and blinking with animation, and on his coarse face a smile so wide and insistent that she could feel her lips and cheeks begin to mirror it—as though acknowledging a bond between them. A hand scooped in under her diaphragm and hollowed out her upper abdomen and a stroke of red lightning slashed through her head from temple to temple just above her eyes. Their smiling at each other was a nightmare version of that exchange between her and her granddaddy in the park so long ago, so very long ago.

Tom was looking down fixedly. Ava moved nervously away, shaking her head.

"Please don't do that," she said, her voice thin and faint.

"Do what?" He looked up, blinking with surprise.

"They're just legs. I don't want to be looked at that way. There's been a misunderstanding if you came here with that in mind."

He chuckled. "They're not *just* legs. They're girl legs. Nice, trim girl legs. Only what I was debating about was the galoshes you've got on. It looks like you're set to go out."

"Oh!" She laughed foolishly, looked down at her feet. "I *was* out, that's why I've still got them on. I forgot all about them."

"Don't you ever worry about the other. I respect your wishes on that subject. What I'd hoped was that we could have a little talk privately to get acquainted with each other. Then if things turn out one way, I'd ask you to have dinner with me and take in the show at the Mapes or Riverside. If it turned out the other way, I think we shouldn't ever be seen together in public."

He talked slowly, quietly, watching her. She listened, half-nodding.

"Understand?" he said.

"We'll talk. The closet's right there if you want to hang up your coat. I'll get these galoshes off and make us some coffee."

"That sounds fine."

Ava set a plate of sweet rolls on the dinette table, put water to heat for coffee. He was wearing a suit and tie this evening and looked less rowdyish than he had at the craps table. He came over to the dining area and watched her with an amiable smile.

"If you'd like to sit down . . ."

"Thanks." Seated, he said, "I like strong coffee."

"Strong as you like," she said, putting a jar of instant coffee on the table.

"Significant remark, Ava?"

"What?" She looked at him blankly.

"'Strong as you like,' you said. Referring just to coffee?"

"Just coffee." She looked at him thoughtfully. "You surprise me. I'd expect you to be completely literal-minded, and not try to interpret simple remarks as something complex. You seemed more . . . down to earth . . . more realistic." Her brown eyes clouded.

"Don't cry, baby, don't cry," he crooned laughingly. "I'm still the man to master you even if not the complete primitive you thought."

She brought the hot water over, poured it into their cups, looking peevish. When she seated herself she said primly: "I thought it was understood that I'm not looking for a man."

He nodded, smiling, watching his coffee as he stirred it. "Understood."

"Then why did you make that silly remark about my looking for a man to master me?"

"Just talk. Didn't mean it sexually. Forget it," he said casually. He sipped his coffee, nodded approvingly. "Just right. You can't get anything but weak coffee around the casinos. And they're always pushing liquor drinks at you. Weak coffee so you don't get alert; strong drink so you'll feel loose with your money. They've made larceny a fine art; no detail neglected. They're smart. You have to be smart to beat them." He helped himself to a sweet roll, took a bite and chewed, his bulging, amber eyes watching her amusedly. "Smart like you weren't. We can't get by with anything that crude again." He reached into the inside pocket of his suit, tossed an envelope across to her. "I gave you twenty. My total profit at the wheel was three hundred. The other two-eighty is in there. All for you, Ava."

She pushed the envelope back toward him in annoyance.

"Listen," she said, her voice low and husky. "I didn't really know what I was doing. I didn't remember till about an hour ago that it was really twenty-four not twenty-five that you bet. As I said in the casino, I was half-asleep. But it was more than that."

She passed her hand nervously across her eyes. "I was totally blanked out. I didn't even remember your coming to the table or the other player leaving. I didn't remember a thing we said to each other, not till just a while ago. I don't suppose you'll believe that; I can hardly believe it myself. All I remember was coming to when you yelled at me that you'd bet on twenty-five and for me to pay you. You bluffed me, and maybe some unconscious part of me knew what was going on and wanted to get involved in something dishonest like that, but I didn't know it. I don't want any part of that money. I wish I could think of a way to get it back to the casino. Maybe I'll just return the whole three hundred and fifty and tell them I made a mistake in a payoff."

"Admirable little speech, Ava. I suppose you've guessed by now that I'm a detective." His tone was abruptly harsh.

She became rigid and staring. He took another roll and began to eat it, a gloating look on his face. He washed down the roll with coffee, reached over and tapped her under the chin.

"Close your mouth. I'm not a detective. And unclench your bottom. You're sitting three inches taller than you are."

It was almost literally true. She relaxed, sinking visibly onto the chair. She looked down hastily, tried to lift her coffee cup, but the coffee sloshed into the saucer. She got up hurriedly, brought paper napkins and busied herself blotting the saucer, her eyes downcast.

"It's all right," he said soothingly. "I don't want to scare you any more than necessary. But you had it coming. You admit it was pretty stupid of you never even to have considered I might be fuzz. Don't you?"

He waited. She kept her eyes down, compressing her lips stubbornly.

41

"Stupid, wasn't it?" he repeated.

She nodded, sat down dejectedly.

"All right. Now, let's ease off. Here, eat a roll and drink your coffee and have a cigarette. Then take the money and enjoy every penny of it. I knew you were in a dopey condition and I played you along like a puppet. It wasn't your fault at all. That's my specialty, influencing people. I can take people in full possession of their alleged wits and separate them from great gobs of their most cherished possession—money. Now don't you think a minute about turning that money back in. They're not quite down to their last million. If you told them you made a mistake like that and explained how you were 'blanked out' what do you think they'd say?"

She shrugged. "I don't know."

"But what do you think?" His voice became surprisingly gentle. He smiled coaxingly.

"Well—they've always been decent to me. I'm not really a very good dealer, but they've kept me on. I suppose I'd get a warning to stay alert."

"How long have you worked there?"

"About a year."

"You've been warned to stay alert?"

She shook her head vigorously. "Nothing like last night ever happened before. I never blanked out or . . . or . . ."

"Cheated," he said for her. "Never?"

She looked at him gravely and lifted her right hand solemnly. A corner of his mouth twitched in a half-grin.

"Honest to God!" she cried.

He held up a protesting hand, saying "I was laughing at myself. Because, against my principles, I *do* believe you. Just idle curiosity, Ava, but what're you doing out here? How come a house pet like you didn't head back for the Midwest after your divorce?"

She looked at him in alarm. "How do you know so much about me?"

He winked. "Magic. Black magic. I'm an evil genius."

She shook her head, pushed back nervously at her hair. "Do I know you from somewhere else?" she asked, barely aloud, staring at him.

"You don't recognize me at all, then?"

He looked at her intently. She bit her underlip, stared helplessly at him. "I know I *should*." She began to shake her head uncertainly, then began to nod slowly. "Now I

42

remember." She gestured gropingly. "It's just that I can't place your name. Tom, of course . . . Tom . . . uh . . ."

"Does the name Tom Ignatzingtonthroop ring a bell? You used to joke about it often enough."

She felt a stinging in the corners of her eyes. "Why are you trying to make a fool of me? There's no reason why I should remember you; I never knew you in my life."

"Of course not," he said easily. "From your voice I guessed Midwest. There's a good chance you came for a divorce. Nothing mysterious. Your nerves are shot."

"I *know* that," she cried out. "Why have you come here? To upset me worse? That's what you saw in the casino, isn't it, someone out of her wits you could abuse?"

"Use. Not abuse. My last name's Grebb. I like to be called Grebb. Not Tom. What's your last name, Ava?"

"McKettrick."

"You did come for a divorce?"

"Yes. But I don't want to talk about it."

"You're pretty scared about that blanking out in the casino, aren't you?" She sat rigidly, her hands clenched in her lap, the blood throbbing in her head, and stared at the table. He went on. "Now, you say that if you went and told the management about it they'd merely warn you to keep sharp. But let's try that one again. Suppose it was your casino. A girl comes to you and says, 'Ava, I have this little habit of blacking out—' "

"It's not a habit; it never happened before."

"But you're sure it won't again. . . . Where were we? The girl says she's subject to blackouts during which she gives away a few hundred dollars of the house's money now and then. What would you say to her?" he persisted.

She sat breathing very quickly and shallowly, her face pale, her brown eyes round and staring. She said in a low, toneless voice, "I'm going to scream. . . . I'm going to scream. . . ." She pulled her lungs full.

"Scream your throat raw!" he challenged in a cold voice. "When you're finished, what's changed? Nothing. Nothing but you. You'll be that much nearer the booby hatch is all. If you've got no more guts than to want to turn into a screaming animal, go ahead. You think it'll be a nice easy life in a nuthouse? You'll find out."

"That's revolting—revolting and brutal and vicious, to call a mental illness a matter of . . . of . . . no guts," she said, suddenly furious.

43

"It's nothing else. All nuts are yellow. They can't take pain. They can't face anything. They fail at everything to give themselves an excuse to quit. They can't face their own nature or the way the world runs. They want to get back in diapers and be taken care of."

She sat, leaned forward, her hands clenching the table, her eyes brilliant with anger. "You're a monster!"

He laughed. "We're getting acquainted. Monster meets lunatic."

"I'm not a lunatic, you ignoramus!"

"Just say subject to mental lapses."

"Not that either. I remembered everything—later, but I remembered. I knew what I was doing."

"Glad you admit it."

"I didn't admit—" She broke off. "Well, it was like—like sometimes people get drunk and don't know what they're doing."

"A very good point. They only *claim* they don't know what they do. Fact is getting drunk frees them to do what they want and excuses them afterward. Drunks are one form of loony, and yellow like the rest of them. At least you don't blame it on alcohol. It was self-hypnosis with you. But never mind. We don't want to fight."

She said nothing, just sat, her eyes loathing him, her senses quivering with hostility.

Unperturbed he said: "You know, I've watched you at work several times, Ava."

"What do you mean you've been watching me?" she bristled. "When?"

"Last night around midnight; the night before a couple of times, the night before that. What a personality you've got!"

She sprang to her feet. "I won't take that. That's one thing—" Her voice was low, quivering. She felt dizzy. "I just won't. Get out!"

He spread his hands placatingly. "I like you. I've been roughing you. Now, I want to be nice."

"Nice!" she said bitterly. "You're a sadist!"

"Think I'm jeering? I'm cheering. I admire your personality. In action at that roulette wheel you're a real pleasure to watch. You've got an atmosphere about you. Sympathy. You make the players feel you're with them instead of the house. I watched them. They like to talk to you and hang around you. They sit there and play and play.

It's an invaluable personality. And don't think the casino doesn't know what it's got in you."

She sat down again, studying his face. "You mean it."

"Well, of course! And I think this business of the casino telling you that you're not a good dealer is contemptible."

"They didn't say it. I just know. I'm clumsy."

"What do you mean 'clumsy'?"

"The way I shuffle cards and—"

"That! Mere mechanics! You can develop physical skill; it's all a matter of inner will. But if you're actually clumsy it proves your personality must have unusual value. Why do you think they keep you on—out of the goodness of their hearts?" He laughed explosively. "Hell, no. You're valuable to them—just as you *can* be to yourself. You feel a little better to know you got a nice personality?" he said, almost affectionately.

She smiled down, broke off a sweet roll.

"That's it. Relax. Eat. I gig you but I'm on your side."

She finished the roll, got fresh coffee for both of them. He offered her a cigarette, which she took. They sat smoking, saying nothing, not looking directly at one another. She was keyed up, part aggravation, part stimulation, and she had to bite her inner cheek to keep from smiling with secret satisfaction in his appraisal of her personality. Now and then he put his hand on the table and nudged the money envelope a half-inch or so in her direction, each of them pretending the envelope didn't move. Finally she broke out laughing, pulled the envelope the rest of the way.

"That's the kid," he said approvingly. "You gamble?"

"I'm afraid so."

"Just consider that as a partial refund. You get a bang out of gambling?"

"It's just something to do, but it keeps me broke."

"It's being broke and worrying what'd happen if you got fired that makes you scared. Don't be scared, kid."

"But—"

"You know why people are scared? They want to be. It keeps 'em safe. Know how to cure fear? Do what you're scared of doing. Of course, you may wind up dead," he added, laughing.

"But who doesn't?" She laughed with him.

"That's good. 'But who doesn't!' Now this three hundred dollars. It's nothing. You know what kind of scare I'd like for you to make, Ava? Fifty, sixty thousand. In a nice,

45

untaxable chunk. That much for you. That much for me. We'll do it right under their noses. You pay out the money, I'll collect the money, the casino will provide the money. We hit, split the take, and run!"

Grebb sat forward, watching her with a big grin, his bulging, amber eyes bright with excitement. "How's that sound?"

The blood was pounding in Ava's head. She opened her mouth, shut it, shook her head. "I don't . . . I don't . . ." She cleared her throat. "I don't see *how*."

He reached for her hand, held it and patted it. "It's all right here in this nice little hand."

She freed her hand, folded both hands on her lap. "Do you mean you think I could hit any number I wanted to? With the wheel turning all the time? There's no way of doing that. If my life depended on it I couldn't do it. It's impossible."

"The casino doesn't think it's impossible. Or why would you and the other girls and men on the wheels have instructions to vary the speed of the ball?"

"It's true we're not supposed to throw the same way every time. But—"

"Wait. Let's take this step by step. When you begin a new play you take the ball out of the number slot in the wheel where it fell the last play. You bring the ball up to the top of the slope that encircles the wheel. There's a little groove up there and you start the ball spinning around in that groove. After it goes around seven or eight or ten or twelve times it loses momentum and drops out of the groove, and still circling it moves around and down the slope that leads down to the edge of the wheel. The ball reaches the edge of the wheel, which turns in the opposite direction from the direction of the ball. The ball clockwise, the wheel counterclockwise."

"Yes," she said as he glanced at her.

"The ball is now at the edge of the wheel. In the wheel are thirty-eight slots numbered from '1' through '36' plus '0' and '00.' There are partitions between the slots. Sometimes the ball is batted by one of the partitions, sometimes it, falls against an outer edge, sometimes it bounces in and out of two or three slots before coming to rest in the winning number.

"There are raised obstacles on the surface of the slope

46

and the ball might strike one on the way down or hit one after being batted by a wheel partition or after bouncing out of a slot. The ball's action is wildly erratic. The whole thing is chaos. Impossible to predict where the ball might finally settle, since the wheel continues to move all the time. Therefore it's hopeless and we give up. Right?' '

She turned up her palms. "I don't know what else, I really don't."

"What we do is break everything down into individual parts. There is only one point at which we have any influence, which is, of course, the throw of the ball. This can be varied, depending on the force with which you propel it."

"But that's just it, I can't control that—even if it would do the slightest bit of good, which it wouldn't."

"One step at a time, Ava. One step at a time." He set the bowl of his spoon on the edge of the plate of rolls. He took her spoon and lay the handle on the edge of the plate about a third of the way around the circle.

"My spoon is the point at which the ball starts on its spin around the upper groove. The ball goes around and around, then, losing momentum, leaves the groove at this point," he touched her spoon. "Clear? Good. We'll assume that the ball went around ten and one-third times. We'll assume that instead of your arm and hand throwing the ball that we have a mechanical arm attached to a little machine. The mechanical arm can be adjusted to exert precisely the same amount of force on each throw. Each spin will begin here—where my spoon is—and come out of the groove there at the point on the circle represented by your spoon. Under ideal conditions the force being the same, the starting point being the same, the number or circuits being the same, the ball will always leave the groove at the same place, assuming we have a perfect machine. Right? This proves what? Nothing, yet.

"Let's look at the turning wheel. At what point on the circle is a given number at the split second when the ball is started on its spin? Let's take the number zero and pretend it is at the same point on the circle as the starting point of the ball. Now let us follow zero around and around and around and see where it is at the end of the ball's spin in the upper groove—where zero is on the circle

47

when the ball is at your spoon. At this stage we can only guess, but later we can calculate where zero will be because we can time the wheel.

"I know you'll object that the wheel doesn't move at a steady speed; sometimes you reach in and give it an extra push or two. On the other hand the wheel tends to settle down to a certain speed and because of the way it's balanced, and barring abrupt extra pushes of the wheel, its rate of turning and its rate of deceleration can be computed. This part of the job is too technical and you needn't worry about it. Anyhow, you're beginning to see that if we have a known force spinning the ball and have a known speed of the wheel and can establish a relationship between ball and any given number in the wheel, there is much less unpredictability than we originally thought."

"I begin to see. But even assuming I could learn to control my throw—"

"Forget the mechanics; forget whether you can do it or can't. It's not a matter of can or can't. It's a matter of will or won't. If you won't, you can't. If you will, maybe you can't either, but on the other hand . . . Intrigue you?"

"It's fascinating, really. It *seems* hopeless, but—"

"Challenges you, doesn't it?"

She considered, her eyes blinking rapidly. "Yes, it does. Oh, I want to be involved. You really think it can be done?"

Grebb winked at her and said very slowly, very softly: "I really *know* it can be done."

"Honest?" she said, watching him closely.

"Dishonest."

Ava giggled. "You know what I mean."

"It can be done. It has been done. Don't ask names, dates, places, amounts. But I've trained girls. I admit they didn't have your problem of clumsiness. I say you have no such problem, really. All in your mind. I can watch a fighter walk and judge his punch; I can tell plenty about a woman by her walk, too. In looking you over the past few days I saw that your co-ordination's good. The way you place your feet, swing your arms, carry your shoulders and head spells fluidity. In turning a corner, weaving through a crowd, you're always in easy balance. You're small-boned, delicately made. How could your hands be an exception to the rest of you? They aren't. I played your wheel. There was no fumbling or lack of nimbleness to your fingers."

"The way you've been watching me makes me feel—stalked."

He grinned. "I'm a helluva good hunter, Always have been." He looked at her with a little too much satisfaction.

She felt a beginning blush and said hastily: "You really didn't notice any clumsiness about my hands at the wheel? That's funny."

"Funny? I had the sign on you. Made you hypnotize yourself and give your best . . . to me!" There was a rough playfulness about his tone.

She stirred on her chair, shaking her head faintly. "My hands did used to have a lot of co-ordination." She looked at her hands impersonally, moving her fingers. "I played the piano almost all my life. I was a star pupil in a lot of recitals. For a while in my early teens one of my teachers talked seriously about my making a career in music—as a performer, I mean. But trying for the concert stage would have been too grueling and it would have led me too far away from the kind of life I wanted . . . a quiet kind. A quiet life!" She gave a short laugh and shook her head. "Imagine my being here, getting involved in this kind of thing!"

"With a man like me, you mean?"

"Yes. What," she said hesitantly, "sort of life have you had?"

"I was born young, spent some time in boyhood, became a man and found a girl with a musical background and enough manual dexterity to earn us a hundred grand. Am launched on the task of teaching her to unkink her mind so she can use her hands for her own purposes. I'm sure you got a gold star at Sunday school, *your* daddy had credit at the bank and *your* mommy grew flowers and was fond of culture and everybody was polite to each other and thought love made the world go 'round." He smiled. "Hate makes the world go 'round."

"In other words, your life's none of my business."

"The point I made and which an unprejudiced listener would have heard was simply that we're living now, today, and knocking off the roulette wheel is our only reason for associating." He said with elaborate patience, "Of course my not-nice remark about hate making the world go around was given a characteristic treatment—ignored. Monkey hear no evil. That's you. Let me try to drive a couple of facts

49

into your head, because if you're going into this affair with the belief that you're good and I'm wicked, I wouldn't trust you. Not for a minute. You'd crack up; break in the middle; go to pieces under stress. Imagine your being here, getting involved in this kind of thing," he mimicked, his voice low and savage.

He went on with rising scorn and hostility. "You hand yourself a medal, don't you, because you've enjoyed the luxury of being on the side of the mighty and never having had to steal or lie or rob or kill or hate? You think there are good people and bad people, honest people and criminals. You think because survival was handed to you that you're naturally superior to anybody who had to fight to survive. Your kind would like to believe hate doesn't exist, doesn't motivate, or if it does that it's wicked. If you knew your history you'd know you were a liar.

"All your easy living, all your so-called 'culture' and pretty piano-playing were made possible because you had it made, because somebody made it for you. You were on the side of the winners. You didn't have to be "bad" because you had what you needed and wanted, because somebody did the dirty work for you—your father or his father or his father!" He stopped, his face dark with anger and lit a cigarette with shaking hands and whipped out the match.

"War, baby, makes countries rich and strong. It lets them build empires. The profits give them the leisure for beautiful ideas and culture and education and all the luxury that goes with successful exploitation—including their notions about being good, kind and noble. They got there with *hate.* All the high civilizations with their high art got the way they were by hate, by killing and stealing and plunder and by crushing and enslaving the enemy. On a smaller scale it's the story of every man who gets strong enough to be able to talk about his high virtues—about love, about goodness and decency and 'nice' people versus 'ba-a-a-d' criminal people."

The intensity, and worse, the ugly logic of some of his points made her squirm and stare at him in dumb shock. He blinked and waved a hand. "So what the hell! You can't help what you are. But, baby, look it naked in the face and know what you're getting into, and why you're getting into it, and *if* you're gutty enough to get into it at all."

"I am," she said tightly. "Give me a cigarette. I'm shaky, too. An attack like this is very upsetting. I'm not *used* to it."

"You'll get used to it, you'll get tough enough to get used to it, or the whole thing's off."

"I want to," she said, her voice low and throaty. "I want to get tough. So tough that—" She broke off, fanned at the smoke veil between them and looked at him steadily.

He returned her look bleakly, then surprisingly, reached over and patted her hand.

"We'll talk about something else. How do you live? Social life, boy friends, girl friends, et cetera?"

"I read, gamble some, drive out to other towns sometimes. No girl friends. I have a few dates. But no romance. Nothing even near romance."

"Is your ex-husband the why?"

"Yes. In my heart I'm still . . . well, romance is impossible with any other man." She looked away. When she looked back he was frowning thoughtfully.

"I don't know, Ava. You ought to have a boy friend. Let it get serious. Get engaged. To some local kid that's settled here. Any chance of that?"

She shook her head. "I'll never marry."

"I mean any chance of any local kid falling hard enough to want to get engaged to you?"

"I dated one man who's still very interested. He's a lifelong resident. He works in the casino to pay for his education. He's going to be a lawyer, locally."

"He's the guy. Sweeten him up. Let him ring you."

"That couldn't happen without his wanting . . . well, privileges. . . ."

"Stall."

"How could I when I've been married?"

"But, Ava, you've got to look safe. You can't go around advertising you're liable to jump town after the next pay check. You've got to have a front. Like I have. You've seen my front. Loud-mouth tinhorn. I never have operated in this part of the country; I've never been convicted of anything. The fuzz around the casinos have got me tabbed as a strong-arm at worst. They wouldn't want to tangle with me in an alley, but the last thing in the world they'd suspect from me is a subtle operation. And you've got to look like a kid with a stake in the future of this town, with too much to lose to be involved in anything. Now if part of that front involves giving your guy a convincer in the bed, why be sentimental and stupid? There's too much at stake."

"I can't go through with such a thing. I find sex with any other man than my husband revolting."

"Correction. Your former husband."

"Former, yes, but—"

"He's nuts about you, too, huh? That's why he keeps rushing out here and remarrying you, because he can't live without you." Grebb said with sudden contempt, "Get over him!"

"I won't! I can't!"

"You *are* nuts, aren't you?"

She suddenly covered her face and burst into tears. She heard his chair scrape and hunched her shoulders, shrinking from the possibility of his touch. She didn't want any comfort from this . . . this . . . unfeeling criminal brute. . . . He didn't touch her. She heard his angry, thumping steps moving into the living room.

She stared at him, her face streaked as he went to the closet. He came out, reaching an arm into his coat and staring bleakly at her.

"I can't stand living faucets." He came back to the dinette table, glared down at her. "Forget everything. And I warn you, if you're insane enough to go blabbing about the money you paid me last night and try to get me into trouble—"

"It wouldn't get you into trouble if I squared *myself*."

His fist came at her head like a club, knocking her off her chair. She sat on the floor, horrified, her hand to her cheek, her face wet. He came and stood threateningly over her.

"You aren't going to turn that money in; you're not going to say one damned word about it. Are you?"

She shook her head urgently, panic churning in her insides. "No. No. I won't."

"You're scared now. Don't get brave down there at the casino. If you open your mouth, I'll get you. Afterward, I'll get you. I'll break you up. I mean it."

He turned and walked to the door. Ava cried out. "Wait," and scrambled up to her feet. She ran after him. He stopped, his hand on the door.

"Don't go," she whispered. "There must be some other way we could work things without my having to betray m-m-m—" Her mouth began to quiver.

"Betray who?" he said coolly. "That goddamn ex of yours?"

52

"It's just," she pleaded, "that I *can't* bring myself to do it. . . . It makes me *sick!*"

"You *are* sick." He tapped his temple. "Up here. Sick. Stupid. A nothing. Sorry I've wasted a minute on you. I thought you had possibilities. But you haven't. I can pick up a hundred *smart* dames. *They'll* follow orders. Working with me, that's Rule A Number One. Follow orders to the letter."

"I'm nervous and upset, and . . . and. . ." She nodded, staring up at him with stark eyes, her mouth quivering, and tapped her head. "Like you say, sick up here. . . . It's—oh, my God, please don't say I can't make good at *anything!*"

He slapped her face with his right hand, then his left. He punched her in the stomach and in the chest, light but painful blows. She backed away, but he kept hitting her with increasing force. Against the wall, he smashed his fist into her ribs so hard that she slid to the floor thinking she would faint.

He stood watching her. She got to her knees, to her feet. Her heart was beating violently. There was an intense throbbing in her lower stomach. She reached up and slapped his face. Immediately he hit her. She bit her lip, moaning, and slapped him again. When he punched her with his fist, her fingers went to the buttons of his overcoat, a wild excitement in her.

"Stay," she whispered. "Stay."

He grinned wryly at her and went over to the closet, taking off the coat.

Ava went over to the sofa. She lay on her back, pulling her dress up, her eyes shut, her mouth open and panting.

From across the room Grebb ordered: "Get 'em off!"

Instantly obedient, her hands moved to her panties, her fingers fluttering nervously. In the next instant she remembered an earlier command to do what she was afraid to do and let her hands drop motionless beside her hips in passive defiance. Keeping her eyes shut she waited in the dark for the lash of his anger. He was undressing and didn't notice, but at any instant he would. Her fingers began to twitch, wanting to rush and scramble obediently as her flesh remembered the feel of his slaps and fist blows; the areas where he had struck her seemed to fever and throb with pain.

"Peel. Skin out of your panties!"

53

Ava flinched at the chopping sound of his voice. He was coming threateningly nearer, and her hands lay idle, intensifying his aggravation, she knew. She pressed her stockinged feet hard against the sofa cushion, her toes curling down tensely as if trying to grip. Under the impact of approaching pain she became so overstimulated that her body began to rock slightly from side to side on her hips, attempting in the same motion to contain and deny the raw, wild force within her.

She wanted to open her eyes and she couldn't and she thought this must be a nightmare—a nightmare in which she was in a dark cave. Her mate, her true mate, was coming back to the cave, to his woman, and it was Dave . . . Dave . . . Dave.

Then rough hands ripped her clamped knees apart and fingers dug under the garters of her nylons, the nails scraping at her flesh as her stockings were pulled down to her shins. One thick hand slipped under her lower back while the other dug at her belly, pulling her panties off. Then there was the wheezing sound of Grebb's animal breathing, and her own panting was terribly loud, and she heard the shameful sound of her own voice in a soft, quivering moan. He gathered a handful of the softness of her inner thigh and suddenly clenched and twisted, torturing her flesh savagely.

"Damn you!" she shrilled.

The heel of his hand caught her chin, snapping her mouth shut.

"Don't yell!" he warned.

He was within the span of her thighs and bearing down crushingly. At the moment of contact her eyes flew open, shocked.

"No—it's impossible—"

"Lie still!" His face was above hers, grotesquely distorted.

"I'm not large enough!" she protested. In sudden passion she fought him, jolting her midsection upward and kicking, trying to thrust him off. She hit him in the face and chest with her fists. He cuffed her head and mashed her flat under him and laughed.

"We'll make it!"

He began to force his possession of her. It was slow. The powerful muscles of his legs and abdomen and chest and arms strained, and she continued to fight him. Now

54

and then when she gasped he paused and waited, quivering and panting. Then he began his amorous advance again. Soon he was sweating and so was she and all her passion was spent. When he had completely dominated her and lay grinning with triumph she gathered saliva and pursed her mouth to spit in his face. But he buried his face against her neck and his body began an abrupt, swift rhythm like a seizure that stormed her with a rushing, jolting, overwhelming force.

His male invasion aggravated sensitive, hidden nerves, brought alive muscles inside her which she had never known existed. It was as if these muscles were roused to repel the fiery intruder, their sheaths closing against him in violent spasms and waves.

His intensity rose to a violent peak. Ava set her will against the rush of her own aroused senses, determined not to lose control. Then it was happening . . . it was happening . . . and she felt herself being carried closer and closer to the line separating pain and protest from ugly pleasure.

The acuteness of her physical sensation was beyond pain; abruptly the guard around her mind snapped. With raw awareness she knew the true nature of the clenching action of her aggravated intimate muscles; an excitement in her flesh, an erotic titillation—not a repulsion of the invader but a clinging and embracing. Then she was sweeping across the line, helplessly out of control, experiencing a rapture such as she'd never known—a rapture made more bountiful because she was exultantly aware of the vigor and power draining from him, and she had an exquisite sense of female triumph over him.

Fortunately there was no lingering aftermath, no word or touch of affection. When Grebb had taken his satisfaction of her, he got up at once and groped toward the light switch. But Ava knew that he'd enjoyed her. Smiling in the dark as she went to the bathroom to cleanse herself, Ava thought contentedly that Grebb imagined he was using her. But at a deeper, more realistic level she, the weaker, was using him for her own purpose.

55

Five

Ava freshened herself, combed her hair, came out of the bathroom barefoot and picked up her limp nylons and crumpled white panties. Grebb, back in his clothes, glanced at her and went in the bathroom.

She was standing with her skirt up, putting on fresh panties when he came out. He watched, grinning. She looked at him indifferently, finished without haste and sat down to put on fresh nylons. When Grebb offered a cigarette, she paused, took a light, then continued putting on her stockings. He stood smoking, watching her.

"You okay?"

"I'm okay."

He wandered away, walked back. "Sure you're all right, Ava?"

She stood up, watched herself stepping into her shoes, then looked at him.

"Don't I look composed?"

"You *look* it."

She drew on her cigarette, exhaled and extended one hand.

"Does it tremble?"

"Steady as a rock," he acknowledged. "I hand it to you. I really do."

She shrugged. "Who'd have thought *you'd* be the nervous one," she said with a short laugh.

"Yeah, who'd have thought it? But you were afraid sex would make you sick with anybody but your ex."

He put a nasty emphasis on the "ex"—not from jealousy, but because he resented anything that challenged his arrogant mastery. He studied her as he jabbed out his cigarette. He lit another and waited, wanting her to bring her love out of her private sanctuary into the open where he could attack Dave with scorn and contempt and anger and try to force her to betray, but she wasn't going to let it happen.

"Yes, I said sex would make me sick with anybody else,

but you told me it was a stupid attitude." She shrugged. "You're right. If it becomes necessary for me to give Cliff Hamilton a true-love convincer in the bed I'll be able to go through with it." She looked at him coolly and he seemed satisfied.

"All right. So that's his name, Cliff Hamilton? He's the lifelong resident, the law student?"

"Yes. And floor manager on my shift. He seems to see in me the same thing you did." She smiled wryly.

Grebb bristled again. "What's the same thing he saw in you that I did, and what's the smile?"

"He thinks there's something defenseless about me. *His* reaction is protective."

"He'll learn." Grebb laughed. "Tonight, you start to work on him. I won't come around the casino, but you can begin on him, and also on your throw. Watch how you do it. Count the number of circuits the ball makes on your long, medium and short spins. Get aware of what you're doing; that's the first step."

"I will," she said, nodding, but there was a pucker of doubt between her eyes.

"I told you it *has* been done."

"I know, I know," she said distractedly. "But I can visualize that wheel in motion and the obstacles on the slope and the way the ball sometimes jumps all over the place, totally unpredictably. The idea of ever getting to the point where I could hit one slot out of thirty-eight in that moving wheel—"

"You don't have to." He gave her a grin and a wink. "You won't be aiming at one-*thirty*-eighth of the wheel, but at one-*eighth*. A little more than an eighth. The play won't be on one number, but *five*. Five numbers side by side in the wheel. That's a reasonably big target. What's more you'll only have to hit two times out of ten to give us a winning system."

"You mean ten plays, betting five numbers each play? Fifty units bet? Two wins at thirty-five to one gives seventy?"

"That's it. Think of it this way. The law of averages will hit that one-eighth of the wheel once in eight spins. Twice in sixteen. Two hits in fourteen at thirty-five to one breaks us even, two in thirteen we're ahead. . . . Now all you need to provide is *one* extra hit, beyond the average, once in eight or ten times. See?"

"Yes, I see, but that would be awfully slow, and to make the kind of killing you said—fifty or sixty thousand dollars apiece for us—would require terribly large bets and there's a house limit, you know."

"I know. Obviously we're not going to make it on dollar bets, and the percentage of two wins in ten plays is cutting it thin. In fact, though, you'll achieve an accuracy, over a period of ten or twelve weeks, of three or four or even *five* out of ten. How finely we can hone your throw depends mainly on you. And, of course, big-money play and consistent big-money wins, with you at the wheel and me collecting, if it extended over a long period would be sure to attract suspicion. It would get you canned and me beat half to death." He paused and chuckled. "So we'll operate in a certain climate. A big-money atmosphere. We won't attract the attention we would otherwise during one of the big conventions coming up early this summer. The house limit goes off during that big-money convention play. We'll make our big killing in *one* session. Between now and then you're going to become one of their best and most trustworthy croupiers!"

"I hope. . . . It's getting late. I'm due for work."

"Ava, I'll let you in on something else."

He stepped closer and lowered his voice and his eyes were bright with excitement, and she found herself quickened, his mood of conspiracy affecting her very heartbeat as if she had just exerted herself. "Things will be happening around the Fourleaf Club. They're going to be hit and hit hard on the dice tables, on the blackjack deals, the slot machines. They're not making any money to begin with and they've got big loan payoffs that are hurting them, too. When I start to hit their tables with some of my boys they're going to be staggering! Then they'll begin to fight scared. They'll be half-suspicious of all the help. And that'll be fine."

She broke in, her voice hushed. "Some of the boys?"

"I'm not just Tom Grebb, sweetie. I've got plenty of muscle and bankrolling behind me."

Her eyes and mouth circled almost comically. "Oh, my goodness!" she cried. She dropped her voice. "Gangsters?"

"What the hell are gangsters?" he said exasperatedly. "You let a word scare you! You think *rat-a-tat-tat* machine guns, corpses strewn all over town. How many gang killings are there per week, per year? Not a handful compared to the Sunday morning slaughter by loving spouses. Forget your conditioning. These people are mainly gamblers. They've operated their businesses in states where it's not respectable. You move the Fourleaf Club a few miles west into California, and you yourself are in an illegal business, part of a crime mob—the geography makes you a good citizen.

"The people I'm in business with want to get in on the nice legalized pickings in this state. Only it's rough to get a license, what with the cops and politicians siding with the established casinos. My people have tried to buy in, only the ins won't play nice. So we'll play the way we have to. The Fourleaf Club is going to get slugged in the pocket-book so hard they'll be damned glad to sell out. I'm in charge of operations. But, Ava, the deal between me and you is my own private play. The bankroll boys don't know a thing about it. You won't have anything whatever to do with them."

"That's a relief."

"So just forget them. I'm breaking with them, anyway, once you and I have made *our* score."

"But, Grebb, if the casino is in a bad way financially and your 'hitting' them worse makes them start to fight scared, as you said, and makes them start mistrusting the employees—what about my job?"

"I expect that by the time of the big-money convention play you'll be one of a small handful of people they can really count on. The shadow of suspicion is going to miss you." He grinned. "We've got ways of casting the shadow on wrongos."

"You surely don't mean you'd get anybody in trouble deliberately? That's so unjust to innocent people."

"Nonsense! They'll get other jobs. Worry about yourself! You're going to be in a position to handle that wheel on the big-money play. As this Cliff Hamilton's fiancee you'll be above suspicion. If they've got too many good croupiers that they trust, you might get bumped off the wheel at the wrong time. It's them or us. I'm with us. All the way. Are you? You said you want to get tough. Changing your mind?"

"I . . . I . . . ." she fumbled.

"Spit it out!"

"No, I'm not changing my mind," she said tonelessly, looking past him.

59

Grebb went over and got his hat and overcoat. "I'll push off for now. You get on downtown to work. I've got to go to Frisco. I'll be back and in touch with you in a couple of days."

Ava nodded.

At the door, he paused and looked at her with a sort of affection and for a cringing moment she was afraid he might want to kiss her. But he just patted her shoulder and said: "Watch yourself." Then he was gone.

She put on her coat and galoshes, went out to her car and started for the Fourleaf Club.

There was a fair-sized crowd on the main floor and traffic on the stairs leading to the baseball games when Ava entered the Fourleaf Club from the alley and headed toward the left wall and the roped-off entrance of the motionless escalator. Unsnapping and resnapping the rope catch, she used the escalator as a staircase and started up.

Glancing across her shoulder, she glimpsed Cliff Hamilton's head afloat on the crowd. He'd been watching for her as usual and his arm shot up like a periscope and waved. When, without pausing, she smiled faintly and acknowledged him with a little flutter of her fingers, he beamed with foolish pleasure as if he'd accomplished something spectacular. Out of his sight she shook her head, thinking with a certain regret that the very qualities she liked in Cliff—his all-out, totally involved approach to things, whether it was the earnestness of his job and law studies or his high-spirited enthusiasm for pure fun—had about them an unguarded quality, too soft for survival. His protective attitude toward her was touching but laughable because her strongest feelings for him were maternal. As a couple they were the weak protecting the weak. Dates with him, while they could brighten her spirits, seemed childish playing at life, and a serious man-woman relationship was unimaginable.

The dim upper floors, fully equipped for play but unused at this time of year, were silent as she headed for the third-floor women employees' lounge. There was never a complete change of personnel in the casino; men and girls came on and off duty in overlapping shifts almost every hour of the day and night. She was one of three girls due for work at eleven. But there would be several on-duty girls taking a rest in the lounge, she knew.

60

At first, finding her stand-offish and shy, the Fourleaf girls had tried to break through to her. But now they respected her privacy and didn't insist on re-creating her in their own image. Independent and nonconformist by nature, these so-called "lower status" girls had granted her what would have been shocking in the eyes of the smugly self-satisfied "corporation wives"—the right to be herself.

Some of the girls were bawdy, their language profane but good-natured, and almost all of them were easy, outgoing personalities with a taste for sports, parties and, like herself, gambling. Their attitude toward the patrons was tart and cynical, and the "heifer sessions" which Ava couldn't always avoid were rawly spiced with psychological appraisals of players that would curl a bald man's hair. Though Ava rarely contributed anything to the discussions, she'd repeatedly challenged a popular theory often voiced by Mickey, one of the tougher girls, to the effect that women gamblers in particular wanted to lose. They came to the wheels and deals and slots for their beatings because they couldn't get a man to give them their lumps.

"What you're saying is a denial of dignity, as if a woman prefers to suffer."

Mickey tossed back her sleek, platinum-blond head and gave a contemptuous laugh. "The dame part of any dame is a bitch, a cur dog that wags her tail and licks the hand of the man that masters her. If he won't kick 'em around, they turn mean and nasty and kick the hell out of him— and look around for a bull to knock hell out of them. I had a girl friend just like that; she had the sweetest man alive and instead of appreciating him she gave him hell night and day. She met a bastard, a pure bastard who knocked her down and knocked her up. When she got a divorce he ran out on her. To this day she worships his memory. If she was around the casinos she'd use the wheels and deals to kick her around and keep her broke and miserable and happy. Don't tell *me*, dreamer."

"I *will* tell you, Mickey," Ava had cried, becoming pink and agitated. "Nobody wants to be hurt." She stopped when several of the other girls laughed. "All right, all right. I know there are girls who stay with men who beat them up all the time, but they're helpless. Somehow or other they've learned through their lives that they can't win, that they're going to be defeated, and it's a problem of taking what they have to take. When you *have* to take

61

something so terrible that you'd rather die, there's only one way to survive it and that's to find some pleasure in it."

"Your old man give you your lumps, dreamer?" Mickey tilted her cynical blue eyes under the heavily mascaraed lashes.

"Never."

"Maybe that's why you landed out here, because he didn't rough you enough. Dreamer, you're pretty as a dream when you get worked up. I'll just call you Dream." Affection was mingled with contempt in her throaty voice.

"If he *had* beaten me, and if he *had* refused to let me go, my love would have been strong enough to accept it. Because that's the life force, love is. It's *so* strong that it triumphs over pain. It makes the unbearable bearable. Love is big enough for that."

"Love conquers all?"

"Laugh!" she cried. She began to blink, hot tears crawling in the corners of her eyes. "But it does. It does. It's big enough to make even pain a pleasure if that has to be, so that a person can go on and . . ." Her voice broke and her eyes flooded helplessly. She rushed, choked, into the locker room. The others came in, gravely silent and sympathetic.

"I'm sorry, Ava." Mickey leaned over her consolingly, her heavy breasts brushing Ava's shoulders. "Honey, I didn't mean to open you up. Your man, he didn't refuse to let you go, huh? And you're still hooked on him?"

"I don't want to talk about it."

"But Ava, you've still got to face it. Nobody gets any younger. Cliff Hamilton's a nice kid and you're dumb not to move in on him while he's hot for you."

"I suppose," she had said indifferently, her tone and manner again closing against their intimacy, and let it go at that. . . .

The laughter Ava heard now as she approached the lounge was probably inspired by a dirty joke and couldn't have had anything to do with her, but when she opened the door the shrilling, high-pitched female sound, compressed within the room, rushed at her in the opening like a solid force.

Their minds were in bed and they'd have enjoyed seeing a flesh-and-blood man walk in—whether hero, overequipped and oversexed, or a miserably endowed nonperforming specimen that they could badger unmercifully. At worst

Ava's arrival was a letdown. Their excited, distorted faces turned to her, red mouths open, teeth showing, their eyes glitteringly overbright like a ravening, savage pack. Her impression of threatening hostility was fleeting, an emotional carryover from her timid early contacts with them. There was a gleeful, jeering exultancy, a fierce vital quality about them, a primitive femaleness stripped of femininity. There was no sign of the "dame part of a dame, wanting to be beat," but a wild sort of unpretty beauty which struck Ava's senses with a cackling, high-voltage brilliance.

"Here's Dream," Mickey shouted, and others called "Hi, Blondie . . . Hi, Ava . . . Mickey just told a zinger. You want to hear a feelthy?"

I wouldn't mind, Ava thought, and warned herself she musn't outwardly change character. She smiled, shaking her head. "Not now . . . Hello, June . . . Barbara . . . Mae. . ."

Ordinarily their exchange of greetings was casual and reserved. Tonight the surface responses were the same, but unknown to them Ava had stepped through the wall of reserve and joined them, recognizing and admiring their cool, unsentimental attitudes, their fitness to survive. She changed clothes in the locker room and went down to the main floor.

All the games and half the slots were getting a good play when Ava made her way across the floor to her roulette wheel, looking trim in her Fourleaf uniform. As usual when she first came onto the floor, she thought of her slacks as "man pants" and a badge of failure as a woman. But the thought was mere habit, stripped of emotional tone. She felt almost no tendency to shrink or cast her eyes down. There was the subtlest reshaping of her solemnly pretty young face as she smiled inwardly and the tune of *The Eyes of Texas* ran through her mind to the words, "The eyes of Tom Grebb are upon you."

Though there was no difference in her manner of moving, she weaved among the crowd with a Tom Grebb inspired consciousness of her own grace, balance and co-ordination. She knew that the somehow different tone to the crowd, the unusual, noisy brightness of the casino was actually a change in herself. She had a shimmering, quick-vanishing image of herself naked and bound hand and foot while Grebb dry-scrubbed her whole body with heavy sandpaper, scouring away the invisible shields that had muffled her senses. In a way that's exactly what he had done and as a result she was able now to feel the pulse of excitement in the atmosphere as if she were receiving clearly signals she had scarcely known existed.

A dozen people stood watching and kibitzing the half-dozen bettors at her wheel. Almost the whole betting layout was covered with singles and small mounds of chips of several colors, along with a few silver dollars and one paper-money bet. The action required two people to handle the play: Herb Nard, his tight thin face and green eye-shade giving him the look of the old-time pro that he was, handled the ball, most of the rake-ins, chip sales and pay-offs. Marissa Lopez, a plump-faced, bright-eyed, friendly girl, was beside him helping speed up the play, alert against "late bets" after the ball slotted. The other three employees within the roped enclosure when Ava let herself in behind the wheel were there temporarily for her check-in. There was the uniformed guard; the "ice cream man"—the assistant cashier with the money cart; and helping him with the chip and cash count, Cliff Hamilton.

Ava exchanged greetings with all of them, including Cliff, who was in his mid-twenties, tall and, according to the other girls, very good-looking. At the moment he was looking vaguely harried and his smile and greeting were absent-minded. While she was signing the receipt form she couldn't help thinking with amusement of him as her future fiancé, her front and symbol of stability and honesty, and she smiled so broadly that Cliff did a double take and grinned at her lingeringly.

"I see I'm getting to you," he murmured.

"Wouldn't you be the first to admit you're irresistible?"

He half-frowned. "You don't really think I'm conceited."

"How," she teased, gazing up at him flatteringly, "could I possibly mistake your natural pride for conceit? You swim like a fish, ski and jump like an Olympic star, hunt like Dan Boone, slay all the girls, take honors in your studies. If you're forced to admit all these things, loudly and frequently, does that mean conceit?"

He laughed. "I'll tend to you later."

"When?"

"I'll feed you at three ayem."

"That's a date."

He moved off with the guard and the man from the cashier's office and Ava turned to the wheel. One of her regular players, an elderly, jowly man with asthma, had

64

been watching her and when she took over the wheel from Herb Nard he whopped, "Here comes my luck! How's the girl, Ava? They've been treating me bad."

"I'll see if I can't fix that. You want sixteen, don't you?"

"Sweet sixteen!"

She laughed with and at him, and then looked interestedly from one to another of the players while they placed new bets. When any of them would glance at her, as if seeking encouragement for his or her particular bet, she smiled warmly. She was in the habit of noticing the pattern of play of all her players and after a series of losses involving the purchase of a new stack or two she conveyed to them a sense of regret and sometimes remarked that their number or corner or section was bound to come up.

Obviously, as Grebb had made clear, this sympathetic involvement with their fortunes was an asset to the house. Her seeming to be on the player's side of the wheel, while genuinely felt, always worked to the advantage of the house in the long run—which made her a Judas goat or whore or something, she thought, plucking the ball out of the wheel and sending it on a long spin.

For the first time her attention was divided as she attempted to count the ball circuits and maintain a feel of personal contact with her players. After several plays she felt she was accomplishing neither Grebb's will nor the house's.

She scanned the board and the players as usual, maintaining as much as possible of her normal manner with them, but felt her own insincerity, and was conscious of using her personality deliberately.

Another player began to play, a player without chips or money or body or blood, and she stood transparently between Ava and the real players and her calculating eyes and chill-lipped smile mocked her and it was Sal Jennison, who had been Dave's horrible and then admirable example of a woman who used her personality as a precision instrument. Of course, she was not here, physically, but her spirit was here and everywhere, and where once Ava's whole instinct had rebelled against violation of personal relationships, she was now being embraced by and merging with Sal Jennison.

Ava told herself that her personality at the wheel all along had been an exploitation even though she'd main-

65

tained a blissful ignorance of it. What irony, she thought, as she put the ball into play again, that tonight, launching on this scheme of dishonesty, she was for the first time honest about using her personality. Using it deliberately as a part of the job she was hired to do.

The most disturbing thing to her was that the players responded to her exactly as they had always responded. They liked her; they felt a closeness to her warmth, they saw what was now a deliberate mask of interest and concern and friendliness as authentic. They didn't know the difference—didn't care about the difference. They wanted only the appearance. . . . And that, she thought sickly, was what everyone wanted. If only she had been able to see the truth before, had been able to use herself in a way that had seemed once upon a time to be a violation and falsification of genuine human values, she would not have failed Dave, would not have let her marriage be destroyed, her own life be ruined.

But it was not too late to become skilled in deceit, conditioned to using herself in the way Dave needed. She had not wanted to fight, to engage in what was basically hostility, had not wanted to use her affection and love cleverly to mask and to give outer, civilized form to what was essentially war. But the nature of life, of success, was war, hostility. It was hate. Love was hate's flunky. He had said it, Grebb had said it, ugly and painful and true. *Hate makes the world go 'round.* Not love.

The weakness and tenderness of love could only survive under the protection of its partner—hate. No matter how vile and ugly and tough she must become to protect it, she would make it survive in here. And when again she was Dave's girl, she would not fail him, would not . . . Her thoughts fumbled.

Marissa Lopez laughed beside her and Ava realized that she had spun the ball with such force that it had jumped the table. As the players at the table laughed, she joined them, her embarrassment brief. Confidently she took the reserve ball from the little cup on the spindle above the center of the wheel and started it spinning.

It circuited seven and one-quarter times, she was able to note, and at the same time she successfully divided herself and watched her players and seemed to be rooting with them. Even this small success in double-dealing sent a distinctly pleasant shiver of exultance over her skin.

A moment later the pleasant feeling was replaced by the renewal of pain in her body where Grebb's fists had struck and his paw had tortured the soft flesh of her inner thigh and his maleness had penetrated. The joy of the pain was the greater; it was truer to the real nature of life. It prepared her for toughness, for survival.

Six

Ava had coffee breaks at the lunch counter in the basement at twelve-thirty and one-thirty. The crowds had dwindled by two A.M. and the basement games were shut down.

With the diminished action she noticed Cliff Hamilton's attention centered more and more on her. He continued to spread himself around and made no more than the usual number of stops near her wheel, but she knew he was observing her from wherever he was in the casino.

A few weeks ago she'd noticed him watching her with an obscure, soft smile and during a coffee break she'd asked him: "Why do you smile at me that way?" She'd wanted him to come out with it if the smile was lecherous so she could make it clear there was no hope for him.

"I was laughing at you in a way. The idea of your handling a professional gambling wheel in a casino is funny."

"What's funny about it?"

"I mean incredible. The funny part is the contrast. You look so serious about it, as if you know what it's all about—like a baby reading a dictionary."

"Well, I *do* know what it's all about."

"No, Ava," he'd said earnestly. "You don't. Although you *do*, in a sense, there's another sense in which you never will. To me this is a wonderful quality."

She'd smiled. "Is that what you learn in law school? The distinction between what a person really does, but really doesn't?"

"Yes. Right in the middle of my Rules of Evidence text is a chapter with blank pages. These pages can be read however the student wants to read them. There are passages like that in music, aren't there, where the composer leaves it up to the performer to insert individual variations?"

"Cadenzas. But the avant-garde has gone farther than that. There's one piano composition called '4'33'''—four minutes and thirty-three seconds of complete silence—the only sound is the opening and closing of the lid of the piano."

He laughed appreciatively. "That tops my chapter of blank pages."

"But there really is such a composition. It's been performed for paying audiences and seriously reviewed. It's considered a great listening experience. Just silence. It's part of a new art."

She sipped her coffee, and from the corner of her eye saw him worrying "4'33''" around in his mind with growing annoyance. "Well, I'm sorry, Ava. I'm sorry, but it's absurd. It's outrageous!"

She turned her stool and smiled into his eyes. "I was holding my breath, Cliff. Exactly my feelings."

"What a relief!"

"I was afraid when I said somebody had labeled it art that you'd automatically salaam."

"Listen!" He looked guiltily over his shoulder, then whispered close to her ear, "I don't even like Shakespeare."

"Don't get *that* bold."

"Ava, you make me feel good. We could be and *should* be friends."

"I already think of you as a friend."

He peered at her. "Suddenly I'm nowhere with you."

She blinked. "Why do you say that, Cliff?"

"It's so," he said unhappily. "I can't *build* with you." He frowned and picked up a grain of spilled sugar from the counter, put it on his napkin. "We have lots of little grains like this—a warm look, a pleasant exchange of words, a moment of understanding, of ease in each other's company, a sense of being naturally right for each other, and never an unpleasantness. But suddenly there's nothing!" He shook the napkin. "There's no accumulation. Next time we'll start from scratch again, and we'll go along a while and then suddenly again I'll be nowhere. I'm shut out completely. There'll be that distance in your eyes and I'll be nowhere—like now!"

She lowered her gaze, bit her lip. "I'm sorry if I become

distracted." She touched his hand, looked up pleadingly at him. "I appreciate so much your trying to be nice. I don't mean to hurt your feelings. . . . I'll . . . I'll try to be a better friend."

A week later she'd accepted his invitation to a foreign movie in the college auditorium. The frankly sexual theme of the picture had made her squirm, and in his car afterward he'd tried to kiss her.

"I don't want to be kissed."

"You're human."

"I'm human."

He tried again. She turned her face. "No."

He started the car and drove on sulkily. "You act as if you didn't understand that movie."

"Next date bring along a pack of French postcards," she snapped.

"What are you, a Puritan? Did you go through a marriage intact, or something?" He laughed scornfully. "Some man."

"Meaning *you?*" she blazed. "A man—question mark—who uses a French movie to do his preliminaries for him! That's what makes me sick, your trying to sneak in under false colors—trying to make use of stimulants that aren't part of your appeal, if any. It's as bad as getting a girl drunk or drugging her or something."

"You're just what I knew. A baby."

"Reading a dictionary?"

"Yes. You don't really understand. Nobody but you would think it was a sin to try to stimulate a girl erotically by any means at hand—within gentlemanly reason." He fell silent for several moments. At last he said, very quietly and seriously, "I don't want to do anything *to* you, I want to do *for* you. I want to protect you. The first time I ever saw you wandering, lost, along Virginia Street and looking into every face and seeing nobody, I thought you were the loneliest girl I had ever seen and I loved you, in a way I really loved you, and I wanted you to leave town and go back to wherever you belonged because I couldn't see you without feeling a responsibility somehow. I keep trying to reach you and make things right for you, as if I've been appointed. I have this feeling that you need me and maybe it's not really an erotic feeling at all. I didn't 'specially want to kiss you just now. But I thought I should try to seduce you because my failure to be sexually aggressive might make you have doubts about me." He laughed at himself. "I wanted to give you confidence in me so you'd let me fulfill my mission as your guardian."

She moved close to him and kissed his lips, softly. She gazed solemnly and lovingly into his shadowed face. "Oh, Cliff, you're such a sweet boy, so idealistic, so really fine and decent. I appreciate you and I'm no baby. I'm a woman. But I'm not for you, dear. We're not alike at all. You're young and high-spirited and I'm dreary and very, very old, Cliff."

He had suddenly kissed her mouth passionately. "You're for me, Ava. You're for *me!*"

"No, Cliff . . . really . . . it couldn't be. I'm divorced and I'm not divorced. Your blank chapter in the text on Rules of Evidence explains it. I'm not *really* divorced and I never will be. Till death do us part."

"I respect depth of feeling. And with depth goes constancy and loyalty. Only a woman who hadn't truly loved could easily forget." He hesitated. "It's not late and my family's gone. . . . Why not have a snack at my house and listen to some records? It'll be strictly hands off."

He'd kept his word, but in a way it had been worse, because the mood of it, the quiet, the dim light, the flowing sweetness of the music had made her infinitely sad. One of the records had been dreadfully poignant—he'd played it a second time, trying to get across to her its message— *Someone to Watch Over Me.* But Cliff Hamilton, however nice his intention, was not the one to watch over her.

He was watching over her now, in the casino. Whenever she met his glance she smiled, but very briefly. She never flirted, and to begin such wiles now that she wanted to use him would be obvious. She handled her job and looked as serious about it as a baby reading a dictionary. The look of absorption wasn't put on. She was counting the circuits of the ball as exactly as possible on every spin.

At three Ava left the Fourleaf Club with Cliff and headed down the wide, bright, paved alley toward the Nevacal to eat. It had stopped snowing but gusts playing at their faces and their backs and cascading down from the roofs on either side swirled the dry, loose snow on the ground in veils and circles and shifting, serpentine patterns.

He had a long, loose-kneed stride, his feet feeling out as if expecting uneven ground, then lifting quickly at the moment of contact with the flat surface. She kept pace beside him, her hurried step light. There were few people outside and those few whisked across from the warmth of one casino to another. Neither of them had put on coats, and this sharing of the invigorating weather had a comradely intimacy with no romantic lingering about it. She rewarded his frequent glances with looks of easy pleasure, and told herself she must resee and rethink Cliff Hamilton.

The other Fourleaf girls called him "cute" and they liked to tease him. Sometimes groups of his college friends came in and the girls among them jiggled and giggled in front of him and batted their eyes at him, inviting him to muss them up and itching to get their hands in his thick brown hair. So a cute schoolboy air had surrounded and trivialized him in Ava's mind. Yet he wasn't coy about the teasing; he neither invited nor rejected it but took it casually and as often as not remained aloof from it. He let it be felt that he took himself seriously and maybe it wasn't so that he lacked a vague something that she thought of as "authority."

He could head off or move into troublesome situations in the casino, handling an explosive loser, a bad-tempered or pugnacious drunk with whatever firmness required—including a fistfight at least once. He'd looked comical that time, swinging his long arm like a scarecrow in the wind, and he'd been knocked sprawling twice, but he hadn't let the guards step in and had actually gone on to win. It was unjust to downgrade him because of the deferential, even tender way he treated her.

Within the space of twenty, brisk, clean-feeling strides Ava experienced a rebirth of hope, a sensation of freedom from the dark fixation on the dead past. She had a clarity and certainty, such as she had known on many occasions with her grandfather, a precious knowledge that life renewed itself every minute. She could feel the positive force of Cliff's loving concern and knew that she could build on it, that her stopped life could begin fresh from this minute, and for an instant she had the strength to acknowledge a stubbornly unadmitted fact: that Dave was a part of her past and could never figure in her future, that there was, in fact, and had been for several months, a new Mrs. Dave McKettrick. Dave's love was a dead thing and lived only as a bright fantasy, like a narcotic, like a disease of the will.

They had been walking twelve or fifteen inches apart and the brushing contact of her arm against his surprised her. She glanced up at the instant Cliff glanced down.

71

"Am I walking too fast?"

"No, not at all."

"When fillies tire they don't keep a straight course. They bear in or out, but so do colts." He grinned. "Maybe I was creeping over to you."

"No," she said softly, giving him a sparkling-eyed smile.

"You decided to come on over?"

"I didn't know I was coming. I didn't decide. Suddenly there I was."

They reached the Nevacal, a horse-betting club, closed at this hour except for the restaurant at the front end. Cliff held the door for her and she went in, her mouth watering in anticipation of "the best rye bread west of Brooklyn," her nostrils absorbing the bouquet of bacon and thick hot soup and fresh coffee, and the brightness of the pair of horseshoe counters and the dozen or so men and girl dealers from three or four casinos made her blink with pleasure. She was known and she knew many of the others; she was a part of this no-longer-strange scene. The mood and tempo of the city pulsed with vitality; the natural beauty of the surrounding areas gave a richness and variety to life here, to the future. . . .

A thick man was sitting with a sultry girl in a fur coat at one of the counters. Ava suddenly felt as if she had hit a wall which became a circle surrounding her. It was Tom Grebb.

Seven

Grebb was eating from a platter, dunking bread into a soft egg. He glanced at the opening door as he might have at anything moving, and not expecting to see anything concerning him, he didn't see her and returned to his food. An eyewink later he looked up and gave her and Cliff a prolonged, impersonal stare.

He knew her, of course, but there was no flicker of recognition. Ava managed to match his composure though her heart was hammering.

"Let's sit in a booth," she said casually to Cliff.

"Well, there's no booth service. But, I'll ask the counter-man."

She walked over and sat down in one of the empty booths and lit a cigarette and stared into the shadowy emptiness of the horse parlor, aware only, like some stunned, will-less creature, that she was within view of Grebb, who might be watching her.

She heard the counterman tell Cliff in a not-quite-rude, matter-of-fact way that he wouldn't service the booth, and moments later Cliff came over with a basket of rye bread and several pats of butter.

"They're calling the soup minestrone tonight. You want some, don't you?"

She nodded and smiled, appreciating the amiable way he accepted the role of waiter. He returned to the counter and she concentrated on buttering a piece of bread.

Cliff revealed two pronounced elements of the executive and would-be executive personality as she'd observed it—he tried to avoid not only giving offense but taking offense. Grebb, for instance, would have taken instant and furious offense at the counterman's tone of voice. He might have bellowed, threatened, stomped out—at the very least he would have bristled and muttered and glared. Cliff smiled. Cliff was civilized. Not a savage, not a criminal. He moved safely and securely with decent people, not against them.

Grebb looked at her now and then and she could feel, like a spot of rouge on her right cheek, the point where his glances touched, and she wanted to look at him and his girl friend and defy him with her eyes. He had lied to her about leaving for San Francisco. He was not to be trusted in any way. Her whole entanglement with him had been a desperate reaction against despair, an effort to destroy her unbearable identity.

Now that she was free of the fantasy about Dave's continuing love, now that she need not destroy Dave—her thoughts fumbled, backtracked, revised—now that she need not destroy her own suicidal fantasies about a reunion and future with Dave . . . well, now she didn't need Grebb. That is, she didn't need to be hardened to the point where she could do something criminal, something horrible like . . . like the killing, the big killing, in the casino at her wheel.

She was holding her breath and eased it out. Turning, she looked directly and scathingly at Tom Grebb, conveying her scorn and loathing and disdain and total rejection of him and everything he represented. He grinned slightly and said something to the sultry girl in the fur coat, who looked over at Ava for just a moment with a hateful pussy-cat smile.

Cliff brought their soups and settled across from her and beamed on her. "Eat up!"

She took up her spoon and smiled at him with a sweetly docile air.

"That's a good girl."

"Did you know my grandfather was a judge?" she queried abruptly.

"A judge! Really?"

"A Justice of the Ohio State Appellate Court for several years. A very highly esteemed man."

"I should say so, Ava. Justice of the Appellate Court!"

"My parents died when I was very small and he brought me up. Your saying 'That's a good girl' reminded me." For a moment everything blurred. She wiped her eyes and Cliff reached over and caught her hand. She withdrew it quickly. "I wasn't crying. . . . I hate cry-babies. Only, when I think of him I get emotional. He was such a good man; we were so close, so happy with each other," she said dreamily. She smiled at Cliff. "He was tall like you."

"And he was a young law student once upon a time, too. Don't forget that."

"I've thought of that, Cliff, and of other reasons we have for being very good friends," she said lingeringly, then abruptly changed tone. "For instance, we both like this rye bread."

They laughed and began to eat and she thought *I hate you, Tom Grebb,* and she could feel him lurking like a nightmare at the edge of her vision and willed him out of existence and promised herself that the moment he left she would tell Cliff about him, about her own cheating or—she hedged, mistaken—payoff last night . . . and Cliff would notify the police and the guards about Grebb and the vicious bully wouldn't dare take revenge on her.

She musn't say anything now because Cliff would look over at Grebb and Grebb would know what she was saying and there might be a fight, and against such a primitive Cliff could get hurt, seriously hurt.

She had a horrible picture of Cliff floundering and being

smashed repeatedly till his face was raw and unrecognizable, his senses shattered, his bones broken, his nose bloodied, his eyes clawed. She just sat, holding on against the tempestuous assault of images, wanting to laugh at the ridiculousness of Grebb clawing, woman-like. With an impulsive, protective gesture she reached over and petted, then squeezed Cliff's hand and gazed with genuine tenderness deeply into his eyes.

He looked bliss-struck, almost stupified with pleasure at her spontaneous show of feeling for him.

"Ava," he said softly. "Ava. You sweet, lovely . . ." He drew in his breath. "You make me so *damned* happy."

"I'm very glad of that, Cliff. I had to resist you at first. It was a point of honor, of loyalty. You reached out to me and I could feel you as the greatest temptation I'd ever had —a temptation to betray, as I thought of it. You were a symbol of violation of my love. But actually you're more than a symbol. You're you! For the first time since my divorce I'm receptive. I want what any girl wants if she's found the right man. And I think I have found—" She closed her mouth abruptly, shook her head.

"Don't stop, Ava, please don't back away. . . . Don't let everything fall to pieces."

"It's not that this time," she said hastily. "I know I've not opened up enough with you in the past. Now I don't want to swing to the opposite extreme and say more than I really mean. You wouldn't want that."

"I won't rush. But I'll keep pushing."

"I want you to."

They returned to their food. She could see the picture the two of them made, the warm absorption with each other. Grebb, from his stool at the counter, could see that she was definitely making progress with Cliff Hamilton—her face was unnaturally warm—just as he had ordered her to do. And she wasn't sure—she wasn't sure—whether she was binding herself to Cliff against Grebb or for him.

Grebb and his girl were standing up. As Grebb walked the few steps from his seat to the aisle in the direction of their booth, Ava tensed in spite of herself. Of course, Grebb turned toward the door and then she heard it open and felt its draft and knew he was gone but he continued to grip her like a cramp and she realized her spoon was at an odd motionless angle and that Cliff was looking anxiously at her and the memory of Grebb's violence and love-making was rawly alive in her, scalding her with shame and physical pain.

"What's wrong?" Cliff's voice was hushed.

"Nothing." Her glance jumped at him, away.

"Is it that man?"

"What?" She looked at him sharply. She peered at the counter. "What man?"

"He's gone now. The fellow who beat you for three hundred fifty dollars last night."

"Oh. . ." She couldn't look at him. She stalled, twisting to peer at the door as if she thought he might still be there; realized she was flustering suspiciously. She looked narrowly at Cliff, thought she saw a sort of inspection in his eyes. She frowned. "I remember him. It's funny I didn't notice him at the counter."

"He was with a girl in a fur coat. One of the sisterhood."

"You mean a . . . ?"

"Yeah. She's licensed. Works in a house over in the next county. We give her a fast shuffle when she hits the Four-leaf—not that she'd solicit in this county, but—"

"I didn't see them."

Cliff waved a hand as if dismissing the subject. "It's only that seeing him reminded me. I've been putting it off. I thought I'd mention it here while we were relaxed and easy with each other so that you wouldn't feel bad about it, but you really did forget a very important house rule last night."

"I did?"

"When anybody's in the position where he could win over a hundred dollars the casino rule is that there be two employees to observe the play. When he bought dollar chips you should have called for a side girl or signaled for me to stand somewhere near to watch. You see, it would be one player's word against one employee. The rule is to protect the house against false payoff claims."

"I understand . . . I understand that. I didn't think. I—"

"Don't be upset about it, Ava. Please. It's not a criticism, it's just for your protection in the future if such a situation comes up again. I know it was a legitimate payoff, naturally."

Now was the time to say: "No, it wasn't, Cliff. It was a mistake. I caught it almost the minute I made it. He demanded a payoff on the wrong number. I became unsure

76

of myself and he was threatening and I felt scared and I didn't report it."

She said aloud: "Naturally."

"I don't want you to feel this is personal at all. It puts me on the spot. I hate to have to say anything that might get me in bad with you." He laughed. "You know that. You know I'm speaking for management, not Cliff Hamilton."

"I understand that, of course."

"Things haven't been going too well for the Fourleaf, you know. You may have heard. The financial position is wobbly. And the worst of it is that the wolves find these things out and they attack the weakest . . ." He leaned confidentially close. "I happen to know there's a certain underworld syndicate trying to muscle in. They tried to buy the place, through legitimate fronts, but it was no deal. We'd rather fold than let that class in. I say 'we' because, naturally, I'm identified with their interests, just as you are, and all of us."

"Of course. We're all part of the team. I certainly understand a man's feeling for his organization. My husband, you know, was a—still is—an executive in quite an extensive organization. I know the company appreciates a man's identification with the corporation. A man must have special qualities to be able to subordinate his own ego and merge it until it's almost indistinguishable from the company's." She paused, lit a cigarette, her hands quite steady, her mind cool and clear. "That fellow who won from my wheel last night, is he connected with this underworld group?"

Cliff laughed. "That mug? No, no. These are sharp, big-time operators. But a mug like that is a nobody. One thing, though. We're going to have to be on the alert for sharpies. The syndicate may be planning an undercover war. One of the problems we've got to watch on the roulette wheels is arm-readers. These babies work in teams. They keep track of every number thrown by every croupier on the wheel every day till they've got a line on her throw. Every girl and every man has an individual tendency—they hit more than the average on certain numbers, other numbers they hit less than the probabilities call for. It's because they develop a normal throw which tends to become standard. So it's very important to deliberately vary your throw so you won't unconsciously fall into a pattern some sharpie can read."

She looked at him widely. "Oh, I will. I'll be very careful of my throw."

Her phone was ringing when she got home from work that morning, but it stopped before she reached it. It began to ring again when she was hanging up her coat.

When she answered, Grebb said: "If you're not alone I've got a wrong number."

"Why did you lie?" she demanded. "Saying you were going to San Francisco!"

"I am. I'm at the airport now. Plane leaves in half an hour. That why you murdered me with the eyes? Thought I lied?"

"Yes."

"Good. I thought you were jealous."

"I wouldn't even answer that!" Ava declared stiffly.

"She don't give a damn about me; still she was jealous of you. So you could've been of her."

"What did you tell her about me that made her give me that sickening smile?"

"You crazy? You think I'd tell her anything important? I said, 'There's that classy little doll I won off of at the Fourleaf last night.' That 'classy' gigged her; gave her a real inferiority complex." He made a grumbly, chuckling sound. "Forget her. She's just scenery; part of my front, just like the Hamilton character is part of yours. You handle him very nicely, Ava. Congratulations. Only don't give me such a strong look in the future when we see each other in public. He might have noticed."

"He noticed you."

"He did?"

"He remembered your winning. And he reminded me of a house rule about two employees observing when a man might win more than a hundred dollars on a single bet. And for the very reason that some player might make a false claim to a payoff."

There was a long pause. "What did you say?"

"What's the matter?" she said silkily. "Scared?"

"I asked you what you said! Now what did you say?"

"I don't remember exactly. But he's not suspicious. And when I asked him if you were really connected with an underworld syndicate . . ." she paused, smiling. She got the expected reaction.

"You asked him *what?*"

78

"Just what I said. But *he* brought it up. Following the talk about the danger of a false payoff, he told me about the syndicate and that the Fourleaf's alert against an undercover attack. It was natural for me to think he connected you with such a thing, and if he had any suspicions about my payoff to you I wanted to know. He laughed at the idea of your being connected with the syndicate."

"We'll all laugh."

"He said you were a mug."

"Are you gigging me? Trying out your claws on me, Ava? Because if you are . . ." he said warningly.

"Why, isn't that exactly what you want him to think?" she said innocently. "That you're a crude, laughable, loud-mouthed mug, an alley-fighter at best?"

"Don't sneak 'em in on me in that sweet-bitchy way. I don't take that. You know I don't take that. I'll be seeing you!" He hung up.

Of course, he didn't mean now.

She hung up, laughing shakily. She looked at the clock. He hadn't been mad enough to come charging in on her when he had a plane to catch. Her tension began to build. She went to the phone, picked up the handset. She'd better phone the police. He was dangerous. She replaced the handset.

She'd better get out of the place. She looked at the clock . . . fifteen minutes since he'd hung up. No, he'd have more sense than to come and maybe cripple her and ruin the scheme.

After half an hour she knew he wasn't coming and that when he got back to the city he'd have forgotten it. She drew a long breath and relaxed and the next thing she knew she was sleeping in her clothes and it was noon and she was cold.

She loosened her clothes and got covers and went back to sleep and didn't wake till after dark, and her first thought was that Grebb might never come back and she was suddenly sick. He must come back . . . he *must!*

He'd said he'd be gone two days. Two days later he hadn't come. She expected him on the third. On the fourth she became anxious. Cliff had begun to cling like a fly in muggy weather and though his interest had a moon-struck quality that was obvious to the other girls Ava felt him as divided, part Cliff, part Fourleaf management.

She had become aware of her foot, body and arm position

in relation to the wheel at the start of every ball spin and she was beginning to gauge the force of her throw and to be able to guess at the moment the ball left her fingers how many circuits it would make before dropping out of the upper groove. But Cliff's hanging around disrupted even that tiny progress, because under his too constant eyes she had to vary her throws and avoid all appearance of a definable pattern.

On her dates with him, Cliff kissed her a few times but she didn't let them get into a situation where it could become fervent. She easily guided his interest into talking about himself, his studies, his plans to join a well-established local law firm.

She was trying to keep involvement at a minimum, but the bittersweet twist was that it became a repetition of her earliest relationship with Dave and amounted now to a strategy which worked out nicely, forcing him to think more and more of her in a serious, long-range way. There was a certain fascination in it, on the game level, but when she began to doubt that Grebb was ever coming back the meaning went out of the game.

She had two nights off. Grebb hadn't returned. She sat in her apartment, trying to read and listen to music at the same time when in fact she was only waiting, waiting. What had begun to build began to disintegrate and the feel of his grip on her faded like the changing purplish-yellowish bruise he had made on her thigh.

When she returned to work after her time off, she felt herself slipping back into the dangerous torpor and meaninglessness. Cliff and almost everyone else was in a high mood that night. Free-transportation deals had been made to bring in busloads and planeloads of players from Sacramento and San Francisco. New loads of bettors were coming in every few hours day and night. The weekends especially promised a lot of play. Other casinos had been herding bettors in for years, but the Fourleaf had resisted the policy since there was no way to keep the free riders captive and they could and did lose their money in other casinos.

80

Eight

The next morning the bell rang while she was cooking her breakfast. Through the peephole she saw Grebb on the stoop and her heart leaped. She opened the door, her eyes staring, her face draining of color and then flushing. He came in with that quick, wary-animal scan of the apartment. He relaxed and grinned.

"Surprised?"

She nodded.

"Glad?"

She shrugged. "I'm making breakfast. Are you hungry?"

"For you. You're looking prettier." He turned, put his overcoat and hat on a chair, then caught her around the waist and pulled her close. He tried to kiss her. She compressed her mouth, turned her face. He laughed. "That's what I say. To hell with preliminaries."

She tried to twist free. "No! I don't want to."

"I've built up heat for you. If you don't want to, that builds it more where I'm concerned. I like 'em not to like it."

His arms tightened like bands of steel. "Do I have to take them off you again, Ava?"

She twisted slightly, but his arms continued to pinion her against him and she could feel his excitement.

"Don't crush me! I'll do it."

He released her and Ava went into the bathroom. She came out minutes later wearing only her dress and a bra. She stopped and blinked.

Grebb, stark naked, faced her from beside the sofa, displaying his maleness with a flaunting pride. Lusting and impatient he performed a small awkward dance on the spot where he stood, lifting his thick legs in a jerky rhythm like a bull balancing on its hind legs. The ugliness of his hairy, powerful body struck her senses rawly.

Involuntarily she glided one bare foot backward, beginning a retreat. His glittering overbright eyes caught the motion and the grin stretched across his teeth slacked off.

81

He came at her in a terrifying swoop, his outspread hands snapped around her waist, his fingers and thumbs clawing into her flesh painfully. He lifted her and swung her dizzily and hurled her onto her back on the sofa with such force she bounced. Immediately his body dropped onto hers. He pinioned her arms and bore down with his whole weight.

When she was motionless, the resistance mashed out of her, he reached down and deliberately pinched her. She lurched and gasped, glaring defiance at him. When she was quiet he hurt her again, making her jump with pain, over and over. Then, his mastery established, he calmly shifted his position and penetrated her.

He moved himself in the quickening tempo of his excitement, his confidence in his prowess as a lover showing itself in a nastily arrogant smile. As the fleeting pain he had imposed on her vanished so did Ava's brief sexual response. With growing contempt she became aware of his watching for the flush of passion and pleasure on her face which would tell him, like a pat on the head, that he was earning her approval. She remained cold and presently he quit watching, becoming blind and epileptic with his own pleasure.

He didn't get up afterward, but watched her as she got to her feet.

"I don't know if I want breakfast now, or you again." He leered, reached out and spanked her bottom.

"I don't have much confidence in braggarts!" She gave a short, derisive laugh.

He grabbed her leg, pulled her over and tumbled her onto the sofa beside him.

"I'll restore your confidence, baby! This time I want you naked!"

Grebb began to tug at her dress. Ava held her body woodenly. He grasped her shoulders and shook her roughly.

"Limber up."

She clamped her jaw and stared at him icily. He shook her again, leaning his thick, hairy, naked upper body toward her, his face harsh and demanding above her.

"You stink," she said flatly. "You're sweaty and smelly. Put on your clothes and get out of here."

He seized a fistful of her hair and yanked forward with such force that her teeth clacked; immediately he yanked backward, then forward again with machine-gun rapidity

82

that swirled her senses. She yelped with pain, her scalp on
fire as he got up and pulled her upright by the hair. She
flailed her arms upward, clawed at his arm and brought
her knee up sharply, trying to kick. He let loose of her hair
and she fell sprawling to the floor. Shocked and disoriented,
she started to crawl blindly to safety. He straddled her and
grasped her skirt and hauled it upward along her body and
over her head.

He tugged and yanked at the dress and shook it as if
emptying her from a sack. Stunned, Ava lay face down,
her slight body bared except for her bra. He tore at the
back strap of her bra but the material held and her body
came upward. He braced a knee on her back and pulled
harder and the cloth ripped.

He rolled her on her back and flung the bra away. When
her hands moved automatically to cover her breasts he
grunted a warning and she left herself uncovered. Naked
and panting, he stood upright and looked rapaciously down
at her.

Witless with fear, Ava stared up at his towering force
with frantic eyes and saw the rage twisting his face and
yielded again to the blind instinct of flight, rolling away.
He kicked her buttocks and stepped across her, blocking
any further turn. She rolled inertly onto her back. He
walked away and came back watching her malevolently.

Her eyes turned in their sockets, following his every
move, seeing with horrid fascination the ugly fact that his
violence had stimulated him to a high pitch of sexual desire.

He stood over her head, then walked the length of her
body and stopped at her feet. Propped on her elbows, her
neck stiff, her eyes glittering, she warily watched him looking at her feet and lower legs and knees and thighs and as
his gaze paused at her pelvis she felt a painful needle-like
twitching. His gaze moved on up her body and she was
aware that the nipples of her breasts, their pinkness vivid
against the surrounding paleness, were tense, the centers
rising like tiny spikes.

"Get it over with!" she blurted hoarsely.

"Open the sofa into a bed," he said, "and get on it."

She got up hastily, worked swiftly. She got into the bed.

She thought she was prepared. But when he got in with
her and was about to touch her she broke under the dread
of further pain. She rolled away frantically. The next
moment his fists began to batter her. He straddled her back,

half-sitting on her, his hard knees a punishing vise against her ribs as he cuffed her and threatened her in a low, cruel voice. He released her and turned her onto her back and then, imprisoning her hands forced her to caress him intimately. She lay with her eyes closed, faintly sobbing with degradation.

He was seized with new fury and suddenly covered her, forcing himself upon her violently. Under the impact of the raw, new pain Ava sighed brokenly and let her body move with a boneless, unresisting pliancy to his rhythm. There was a passively voluptuous satisfaction about it and then, suddenly, she needed to intensify the feel of surrender. With a fierce joy she coiled her arms and legs around him, embracing this cruel savage with a strange, dark ecstasy. . . .

Later, he lumbered off the bed toward the bathroom and there was a wake of peace. Her body, beslimed with his sweat and her own, lay naked and chilling and motionless as death, her open legs inert, her feet turned out. Her arms sprawled where they had dropped on the rumpled sheet, one hand on edge, the palm of the other upturned, the slim, limp curves of her semi-flexed fingers a pattern of resignation and despair. Her head was rolled to one side, her mouth slackly open with a slow, gluey trickle of saliva issuing from one corner, her cheek webbed with tangled strands of her dark blond hair, her eyes, the brown velvet irises low in the corners, showing as slick-white and sightless as peeled eggs.

Grebb said: "I'm going to shower. Where's a bath towel?" and one of her feet jerked, the toes rising an inch from the bed and falling back and her semi-flexed fingers twitched and stilled and her tongue, half-wedged in the opening of her side teeth, squirmed and lay still and throughout her body other nerves and muscles tugged at her like disorganized gangs of Lilliputians pulling in every direction and then they all quit.

But his words "I'm going to shower. Where's a bath towel?" were there a long time. In fact, they had been there for as long as she could remember and they would probably still be there long after she was gone, as if the total span of her life were concentrated in one moment that lasted an eternity. There were moments of knowledge so intense and all embracing that every answer was made clear, every perspective mastered, and she said a soundless *Thank you, Grebb* because the pain and degradation he had inflicted

84

had driven her into a new dimension outside every previously known boundary.

Whereas she had never fully understood the exaltation and ecstasy of the spirit among ancient mystics who had understod the final reason for the humiliation, even torture, of the flesh, she was now one with them. Like them she moved toward total knowledge of the essential triviality of the world. She understood the restrictions on the earthbound senses and she saw the whole meaning and plan of her life, as clear as print in a book. Everything was there, complete—from her birth to her death in August just five months from now, two thousand miles from here.

She could feel reality slipping away. Her body stirred and she rolled onto her left side and drew her knees up a little and folded her arms across her chest and shut her eyes tightly, trying to hold onto it.

Once in a dream as a little girl she had held the most beautiful and lovable doll in all the world to her breast and while her aunt said, "Wake up, Ava, it's morning," and her cousins had shouted and thumped around, jarring the house, she clutched her real and beautiful doll tighter and woke with her arms empty.

She heard Grebb thumping about in the bathroom and the shower was running. Suddenly she was aware that she hurt all over. Now her reality was fading and vanishing rapidly, leaving not even a clear memory trace of itself, only the elusive consciousness that it was there. And it would not be impossible to recapture when needed.

The exertion of sitting up made her head ache. She paused, head in hands, her body sagged forward so that her lower abdomen rested on her upper thigh like a soft, plump pillow. The idea of becoming fat and losing her figure annoyed her surprisingly since she disdained vanity. Nonetheless she sat up erectly, sleeking the lines of her body and looking down at herself as she tightened the muscles of her stomach. Immediately, like a retaliation, there was movement within her stomach, like a thing alive kicking in protest against the cramping pressure she had exerted.

She got to her feet instantly and stood, chin on chest, staring down at the small but definite bulge she had noticed a week or so ago. Her fingers moved tremblingly over it, then she cupped the pinkish-white convexity in both hands and massaged gingerly. Her eyes were stark. But a tic-like series of muscle spasms in her left cheek jerked her mouth in quick-vanishing half-grins as she remembered the half-funny thing she had thought last week about the unlikelihood of giving virgin birth, even if she had once been Dave's "pretty little virgin with the blushing legs." No man but Dave had possessed her until last week.

She was overwhelmed by an urgent need for secrecy and wariness. Going soundlessly to the closet, she put on a robe. Pushing back her hair and glancing furtively toward the bathroom where Grebb was showering, she drew the closet door almost shut and inspected herself again, half-breathing, alert for the feel of motion, feeling none, knowing there could be none, knowing it was all imagination, wishful thinking, a several-year-time-lag, too-little-too-late, wishful thinking.

She willed her body to relax, her cheeks and mouth to loosen in a smile. Eventually she did relax and the smile appeared, yet she remained tense, separating inner and outer moods, just as Dave had learned to do. He was never out of control or forgetful of his main purpose. And that letter from one of the friendly corporation wives that Ava had gotten at the time of Dave's marriage several months ago, whatever its intent in hinting that it was a shotgun wedding, had been merely silly scandalmongering. Dave, ever ready with protection, couldn't have got caught unless he had wanted to be—not unless the girl in question, whoever she was, had the proper corporation-wife credentials, the requisite social personality.

Ava winced. The fact that she herself hadn't had the irresistible sexual lure to madden his senses and destroy his control didn't prove the second Mrs. McKettrick lacked that power. And, of course, in the last month's issue of the company magazine which Ava continued to receive, there had been that coyly vulgar item:

Our eavesdropping storklet predicts a new executive in the family. Dave McKettrick, Assistant Manager of the New Bascom City plant, is playing it close to the vest, admitting nothing, just smiling and ordering cigars to be delivered Julyish or Augustish.

Even conceding that the other Mrs. Dave McKettrick had been impregnated at or near the time of marriage, storks maintained accurate mailing lists and weren't likely to put a baby in her belly, too.

Ava tightened her stomach muscles, exerting an inner

86

pressure again, deliberately goading the little life to protest, to a kicking proclamation of his existence. Nothing happened. She smiled bitterly. She tried again, this time pushing her fist deeper and deeper into that bulge, testing . . . testing. . .

There was no movement. No life. The only sensation was deep inside her—a sense of liquid movement and cooling moisture. She moved swiftly to the bathroom door.

Grebb was still in the shower. She said shrilly: "I want to clean myself, too. Hurry up out of there!"

Nine

Ava showered, fixed her hair and face and put on a clean pink house dress. Grebb sat dressed, relaxed in the armchair, reading her newspaper. He glanced at her as she went to the kitchen and set another place, and made breakfast. He ate without speaking. She had only coffee. She knew he was studying her, but she wouldn't look at him. Finishing off with coffee and cigarette, Grebb cleared his throat.

"Did I hurt you?"

She stared directly at him. " 'Did I hurt you!' " she mocked.

"I'm sorry."

"Sorry." She laughed tonelessly. "I used to be sorry about things. I lived scared. You're scared the deal's off between us. It's not. So don't be sorry. You weren't while you were doing it, just hating and happy. Hate makes your world go 'round. That's fine with me. Just don't get tender, it's out of character."

"I'm still sorry I hurt you. I feel bum taking on a flyweight. You're no match; you're a soft kid. . . . I got carried away."

"No place you hit me or kicked me will show. So it's all right. You were careful about that."

"I'm not that bad. I was raised hard in a tough neighborhood. You had to make it or get your own ass beat. The kind of girls I knew expected muscle and guts from a guy.

Ask 'em nice for it and they'd spit in your eye. Take it away from them and they respected you. If they thought you took it because you were soft on them they laughed at you. We were all scared of the pretty emotions. So it's a kid attitude I ought to be on top of at my age, and I am a little bit. I honestly have got a soft feeling for you and I'll get as big a bang out of you having fifty, sixty grand to make you spit-in-their-eye independent as I will about my own score."

"Now that I understand your underlying sweetness," she said wearily, "let's get on with it. Don't feel soft about me. Don't think that way about me. I don't want even the remote cousin of *love*. You liked beating me up. I liked the feel of being able to take it."

"That's not all you liked the feel of! Don't pretend."

She smiled, looking past him. "I didn't the first time this morning—just the second. After you knocked me around and proved whot you are. If you think it's the goodness, if any, in you that I responded to, think again."

He blinked, a genuine look of bafflement about his bulging, amber eyes. "You're something, you know that? I never saw anybody toughen up as quick as you."

"Toughen up quick? No." She touched her chest. "The toughness was waiting. Deep, deep down in here. Waiting for something, somebody to—"

"Trigger it off?"

"That's good!" She smiled. "Did you know the Fourleaf has a new deal going, bringing in new business with free buses? That'll strengthen them financially; they'll be harder to ruin."

He smiled, then chuckled aloud. "That's a joke."

She brightened. "Tell me."

"Some of the busloads will be factory workers from plants around the Bay Area making big party excursions. The Fourleaf will cash lots of payroll checks. Some of them they'll wish they'd never seen."

"Worthless checks?"

"That's not the half of it. They'll get cagey about payroll checks. They'll scream for the fuzz in a couple of cases. The checks will be good. The club will be slapped with false-arrest suits. Those are mere snacks in the trouble feast I'm serving the Fourleaf. So the Hamilton character just laughed that I'm a mug, did he?"

"He'll learn."

"How's he doing with you?"

88

"Calm kisses."

"Better let him had a feel or two." ·

Ava got up abruptly, brought coffee from the stove. Grebb looked suspiciously at her and asked silkily: "It agitates you to double-cross him? I noted the cozy mood there in the booth with him."

"I just thought if he feels me any place you've touched me I'll scream with pain." She yawned pointedly. "I took some pills and it's my bedtime."

"You look pale. . . . I guess you need sleep."

As she got up from the chair, he came around the table. She tried to fend off his helping hand as she walked to the bed.

He removed her shoes and put the covers over her and the grotesqueness of these unwelcome tendernesses made her whimper in futile protest. He hovered near.

"Please go now," she said tiredly.

"See you in the casino tonight."

"Yes."

He put on his hat and overcoat and came back. "I'm not close to anybody. I don't treat anybody very good, but I won't hurt you any more." He gazed down at her. "Things will work out. In just a few months you'll be rich . . . and . . . well, think about that. Have a good sleep."

"You do have a soft side," she murmured.

"Yes."

"It makes you look like a clown."

He went out, offended. She laughed and slept.

During the next week Grebb was in and out of the casino in a blundering hit-and-miss way a dozen times while she was on duty. He came with a variety of girls or alone, playing everything from slots to Keeno and craps to roulette on the main floor and basement and seemed to pay no special attention to her wheel or to her, but he got in four or five hours of timing the wheel with a stopwatch. Her long, medium and short throws were undependable in the extreme, one varying from eight and a half to ten circuits. It didn't worry Grebb.

"I'll rig up a training harness for you to control the length of the swing of your arm and you can practice right here at this table at home, thousands of throws, till the feel of the throw becomes pure habit, automatic. You'll establish a long and medium throw. Purely a matter of physical conditioning.

You'll throw at the same speed in spite of yourself, in or out of the harness. That'll take plain dogged work, but it'll come.

"Right now there's something else I want you to work on. Without paying any attention to the throw itself I want you to observe the exact instant when the ball leaves your fingers at the start of the spin. I want you to observe this in relation to the wheel. At the moment you throw, your eye should be on the wheel, on one specific number in the wheel. The easiest to spot will be the green zero or the green double zero. It'll be very hard to do."

The first few times she tried it she didn't even find "00" till the ball was halfway around. Then when she learned to find the number and keep her eyes from rushing around after it, she had more trouble in relating its position to the chrome obstacle.

Of course, she could see "about" where the moving number was, at "nearly" the instant her fingers lost contact with the ball. But "about" and "nearly" weren't enough. The quick-reflex co-ordination wasn't as difficult as learning piano technique, but there was a literal world of difference between the private practice room in her grandfather's house and being on duty at the casino. There was always an audience or the threat of one. Once when Cliff drifted near and inquired worriedly if she was nervous that night, she flushed guiltily, afraid he had seen her eyes flea-hopping around.

But within the month she had not only achieved cool-eyed mastery of that problem but was progressing with her throw, spending all her free time at home "in harness."

The device was a simple leather belt around her body, and a leather wrist cuff to which was attached an adjustable cord. Often she stood in the dark in the harness, moving her arm to the limit of the cord, her hand releasing an imaginary ball, over and over, scores and hundreds of times in a perfect state of machine-like rhythm, feeling an inner calm and confidence that she was moving toward something far more thrilling than anything she had ever known.

Grebb had had a key made to her apartment and sometimes he was waiting when she got home mornings, and often he came in the evening. For two weeks he kept his word and did not hurt her, but when she began to have doubts about everything he lost his temper and knocked her around. The aftermath of pain and distress succeeded in bringing her back to that strange, dark reality and understanding. He liked putting the harness on her and watching her as she went through the motions he had willed her to go through. He was arrogantly hateful but vital to her.

Her control and calm were greater when he sat across from her at her wheel in the casino. He made small bets and big talk, and especially when Cliff was near he boasted to her about big wins in Vegas or one of the other local casinos. He had no system of play except lucky hunches, most of which didn't come off, much to Cliff's satisfaction.

She and Cliff laughed together about the small-time braggart, and when Cliff guessed that the mug was trying to impress her Ava laughed with such delight, so genuinely amused, that Cliff made a gag of it and began referring to the mug as her sweetheart.

"Seriously, if he ever makes a pass at you, I'll break him up."

"I know you would, Cliff," she said, gratefully, gazing up at him with a near-worshipful smile—something which Dave had found appealing, and in ways he was not too different from Dave.

"He's never asked you for a date?"

"He said something in that line. He talked toward a point slightly west of my head. You know how these braggarts do—talk to hear themselves more than to anybody, saying he treated dames right on dates, took 'em out in real style up to the classy joints like the Riverside . . . then he wondered if I'd ever been up there. I cooled him very politely. After all, he tips me when he wins."

"That indirect approach to you confirms my psychological analysis of him. In my position, naturally, I have to be a pretty good judge of character, and these days we use the tools of psychology. To put it in lay terms, he's intimidated by good women. It's why you see him always in company with the sisterhood. He wouldn't dare presume to approach a girl like you."

"Oh, Cliff, you silly."

He squeezed her hand. "In this case I'm not merely making love to you but stating the fact that this sort of man has a basic inadequacy which makes him unable . . . well, to function sexually, except with girls for hire."

She nodded, frowning gravely. "I see. . . . I think it's wonderful that you study more than the mere technical books and that you incorporate modern psychology in your

91

law training. The personnel people in the organization where my husband worked were quite skilled in that line. They were even set up to reshape defective personalities who had trouble becoming part of the group."

Cliff nodded. "Oh, yes, they're doing wonderful things these days."

One warm spring evening when she came on duty there was a character at her wheel whose slippery eyes and secretive, knowing smile and generally furtive air marked him instantly as a sharpie. He was cashing about two hundred dollars in chips before she took over the wheel and she noticed he didn't tip Herb Nard. Cliff, too, noticed, and during a lull around two-thirty in the morning he said, casually: "I wonder why that sharpie didn't tip Herb?"

In the past week there had been an unusual number of jackpots on the dollar slot machines and also "mysterious" breakdowns of about twenty dime slots, and several thousand dollars' worth of worthless payroll checks cashed the past weekend. Also state inspectors had been tipped off that the Fourleaf blackjack deal decks were marked and that the crap table on the now open second floor was carrying loaded dice in the reserve drawer. Lo and behold, as Grebb had put it, that's exactly what the inspectors had found. Worse than this there were rumors of dishonest employees in the Fourleaf, circulating up and down the street and alley. The management and Cliff—and in this mood management and Cliff were one and the same—were suspicious.

Ava shrugged. "I wouldn't know why he didn't tip him. Maybe he doesn't like Herb."

"He won pretty heavily off of Herb, considering he only played fifty-cent chips. He'd like him for the wins. It's not that the sharpie won't tip. He went over and beat a couple of blackjack deals and handed out tips when he quit."

"Blackjack girls . . . Maybe he just tips the girls."

"One girl . . . one man . . . How well do you know Herb Nard, Ava?"

"Hardly at all."

"You never heard anything—any rumors about his honesty?"

She blinked in astonishment at Cliff, then frowned as she suddenly realized that Grebb was back of this.

"No," she said, "I've never heard anything against him.

He's a very good croupier, that's all I know. And," she said with conviction, "I'm sure he's all right."

"He's tops on the wheel—a good man mechanically. He can handle fast, heavy play and big crowds. I'd hate to think . . . and yet that sharpie was obviously a crook, his whole manner showed it. Just the kind of character the syndicate that's trying to ruin us would harass us with. If he was making an undercover split with Herb on his winnings he'd not think about tipping. I know that's shrewd figuring, but it's an unavoidable conclusion."

Grebb was waiting in bed for her later and when she told him about it he rolled onto his stomach and began to laugh.

"So the Hamilton character shrewdly spotted old Creepy for a sharpie and brilliantly deduced that he and Herb Nard were cheating. That law boy is going places!"

"A moron could have spotted that shifty-eyed character," Ava said angrily. "That's just what you figured, isn't it? He had instructions not to tip Herb if he won, didn't he? To throw suspicion on Herb!"

"Herb's in your way, Ava. I told you I was going to bump anybody standing in your way. *You'll* be trusted, *you'll* be sure to handle the wheel for our killing. Now, skin down and climb in; I've been building heat for you."

"It's a dirty thing to do to Herb Nard. I admire your doing what you are to the Fourleaf, but he's got nothing, just his job. If he comes under suspicion and gets fired he'll be blacklisted all over the state. . . . Grebb, it's rotten."

"There ain't no innocent bystanders. It's beat or get beat. Which do you want? What you'll get if you're not in this bed in three minutes I don't need to tell you."

In minutes she was naked beside him in the bed.

"Tell me about love first."

"No."

"Tell me about love! Knife him, baby, you know you love it."

"I don't love it. I hate your spitting on his honest emotion."

"All right."

She looked at him sharply. "I know if I don't tell you, you'll take it out on me later. . . . On our last date I let him go a little farther," she began.

She reported in a dry, completely emotionless voice Cliff's

93

whole approach, his murmured lines of poetry, his whispered endearments, his assurances that he was in love with her. Cliff put his hands under her dress to stroke her legs; he had come to the point of sliding his hand into her blouse to fondle her bare breasts; he pressed himself, fully clothed, against her, and he would have been content to do this for hours, his stimulations and seductions slow, slow and mild. Cliff stayed constantly on the approaches, never culminating anything, yeilding to her slightest pressure to stop, afraid to go beyond any line she drew.

Grebb considered it fantastic and more than a trifle queer; his contempt for Cliff was total. And when she was betraying his love and seeing him through Grebb's mind, she, too, despised Cliff.

Rather, she despised *one* of the two Cliffs.

As she was leaving the bed that morning after a particularly intense sexual session with Grebb it came to her suddenly that there had been two Daves, too. And she hadn't really loved the one of them which had belonged first to his corporation.

She looked down at her swollen belly and felt the little creature in there kicking her violently.

"Never you mind," she whispered, smiling downward and stroking her stomach. "Never you mind. Only three months now, dearest!"

Ten

That evening she planned to spend four hours practicing her throw. At six-thirty, comfortable in sandals, white shorts and a loose yellow blouse, she adjusted the leather belt to her waist, fastened the wrist cuff and stationing herself at the cleared dinette table she set to work with a luminous clock facing her. It was warm, not yet hot enough for the air conditioner and her window was open top and bottom with the venetian blind slats adjusted to provide a small breeze and concealment from outside.

The outdoor light was diminishing, the shadows deepening in her apartment, and she fell into an unthinking hypnosis of simple motion, confident of the value of simple repetition, easy in the lifelong knowledge that practice makes perfect. There was a mild fatigue beginning in the muscles of her right arm which would become, after two or three hours, a burning which in its turn would vanish.

The fatigue was enjoyable. She thought of it as an acid such as they used to cut a design in the engraving plates to form a permanent pattern—though, of course, the actual acid resulting from fatigue was lactic acid, the acid in milk, mother's milk . . . provided by nature as a sedative for the suckling infant, after which sleep, sweet dreamless sleep.

She hadn't put on a bra, since all her bras were becoming tight, and her unconfined breasts moved with a light, sensually pleasant friction against the thin material of her blouse. The small rock-a-bye cradle-like motion of her pelvis seemed to calm the surging, impatient life in her belly as if this were his sleep time. She hummed with a sound so faint it was scarcely audible to her own ears, and remained a sweetly confined, internal lullaby. At seven-thirty the phone rang and she moved, nearly sleepwalking, and answered it and it was Cliff.

"Are you doing anything, Ava?"

"Just reading."

"I'm not due at work till ten. I don't feel like studying tonight. I want to be with you. Can I come over?"

"Well . . ."

"Listen, Ava, I'm sorry about my suspiciousness of Herb Nard last night. I realized you were distressed about it and rather disappointed in me as if . . . as if I wanted to think the worst. But I've got good news for you. I just dropped past the club and that sharpie was in and he tipped Herb a ten. He'd been all set up about winning and didn't even realize he hadn't tipped. It just slipped his mind."

"I was sure it was something like that."

"Of course you would be, but so many things have been happening. Did you know we're being sued in what I'm positive is an entrapment, for two separate 'false arrests,' and three people in the last two days have fallen on the basement steps and the shysters are badgering us with nuisance suits and our bus excursion deal is about to fall through? Well, the things that have been happening are enough to get a man cynical. But you do believe me, don't you, Ava, when I assure you I don't *want* to think the worst?"

95

"How could I think as much of you as I do, Cliff, if I felt you were that way?"

"I'm terribly lonesome for you tonight, Ava. Can't I drop by?"

She shrugged, sighed. "I'm lonesome, too, Cliff."

"For me?"

"Yes, dearest."

"You called me 'dearest'!"

"How long will you be?"

"Fifteen minutes."

She got out of the harness, a small grin spreading more and more widely as the full significance of the sharpie coming back in to tip Herb Nard became clear. Her mildest objection to abusing Herb Nard had been enough to make Grebb back off! She rose on the balls of her feet and her hands clenching into fists squeezed out an exultant little rhythm, left-right, left-right alternately.

She'd brought him low. Grebb, the tough, strong master, had done *her* bidding. He was under her power, as was Cliff. She stood in the dark doorway watching Cliff approach with that loose-kneed stride, a smile transforming his features instantly at the sight of her.

As he came up onto the little stoop he started to speak but she whispered: "Don't talk!"

She backstepped slowly, her pale oval face uptilted toward his, her dark brown eyes focused intently on him. He came in, his expression changing from pleased bafflement to total soberness as he sensed the sultry mood of the shadowy room and felt the warm nearness of her body, pressed delicately close to him.

She gazed up at him, her lips darkly parted and she lifted her hands and caressed the slightly wiry roughness of his close-shaven chin and long cheeks, her touch soft, and then she rose on her toes, as if her whole being was straining toward him and his mouth came down and covered hers and his hands spanned her body, stroking the roundings of her upper back and drawing her so close that her breasts mashed against him.

She moved her lips against his with a hungering, savoring movement and abruptly darted her tongue in against his with a fiery little jabbing motion that roused him. He stood deep-kissing her and mashing her body more and more tightly against him. She usually turned her lower body slightly, absorbing the pressure of his body on one hip and

96

avoiding his more fervent contact, but now she not only allowed herself to be held in full contact, but undulated faintly and pressed her thigh and bare knee forward against his to further heighten and stimulate his passion. He withdrew his lips and stared down at her, breathing thickly.

"Darling. . ."

"Dearest. . ."

His mouth mashed into and rolled against hers again and one of his hands dropped to the seat of her shorts and locked her in against him. It was an uncomfortable position and she turned her face, breaking lip contact so she could get air and worked her mouth distastefully. Fortunately Grebb never kissed her.

Cliff straightened up and after holding her lower body against him for a few more moments laughed shakily and released her. He fumbled in the pocket of his sports shirt and got out cigarettes.

"We'd better slow down. At this pace I'll never last."

He struck a match and she caught his hand in both of hers and blew it out and then unbuttoned her blouse and threw it back toward the sofa. She stood up and cupped her breasts and lifted them toward him and gazed up, mute, compelling, and he looked at her naked breasts, faintly luminous in the shadows and she willed him down, down, down from his height and he bent awkwardly.

His breath hung in a hot little cloud over one nipple and he retreated, puckering his mouth and kissing the rich satin slope with fever-dry lips. He suddenly kissed the nipple and drew it into his mouth and clung there and she held his face there for a moment, then withdrew her breast and guided his mouth to the other breast and while he nourished himself on nothing more than his joy in dependence she smiled and understood him and every man with a sudden and profound loathing. She pushed his head away and calmly unzipped her shorts and dropped them and as he shivered with desire and sought to kiss her again she said quietly: "Take off your clothes."

She went and lay down and opened her arms and legs to him and allowed him to work out his sexual fever—a short-lived fever at best. And when he was done it was as if they had performed a not very stimulating bit of calisthenics.

"You lover . . . you lover . . . you lover . . ." she kept whispering. "You make me so happy."

97

"Darling, beautiful, precious, Ava. Oh, God, I love you. I can't live without you, Ava."

He had turned on his side and he held her close in his arms, petting her and kissing her face repeatedly. Grebb at least had the good sense to quit when he was done.

"Cliff, dearest, I love you, too, more than I ever thought I could love a man. . . . I just *had* to have all of you tonight. I just had to give you all of myself. . . . And I'm not ashamed. I'm glad. You're the most wonderful man I've ever known in my whole life."

"Barring none?"

And such was love. It was not enough that Cliff had what he thought was her love. Oh, no, such was the beauty of love that it would tolerate nobody else that she had ever loved. How tender and noble a passion that would kill not only what might stand in its way now but any loyalty she had ever had.

"Barring none," she said solemnly.

"Will you marry me, Ava?"

"Do you even have to ask? Don't you know?"

He kissed her.

When she was able to get breath she whispered intently: "Make love to me again, dearest,"

"I don't want to tire you out. . . . No, sweetheart, not so soon."

"Oh, I don't care. I don't care about anything. I can't get enough of you. . . ."

He was able to convince Ava that it would not be to her best interests—that sex was far too precious as an expression of love to indulge in promiscuously. He didn't want that to be the important thing about their love. Translated, she thought with a wry smile in the bathroom, it meant he wasn't up to another session just yet.

By the latter part of May she could depend on it that her long throw would circle the upper groove eight times plus nineteen inches before losing momentum and starting down and around the slope toward the edge of the wheel. Her medium throw was six and seven-sixteenths circuits plus one inch. It had been possible to determine the total length of her throws accurately because of guideposts built into the wheel housing. These guideposts were two-inch-long, diamond-shaped chrome pieces affixed to the wooden surface of the slope rimming the wheel.

98

The obstacles were regularly spaced, set alternately vertical and horizontal, and were meant to send the ball into an occasional erratic bounce, but she and Grebb used them as markers, one through sixteen.

Ava had learned not only to spot the position of double zero at the moment her throw began, but to control the point at which the ball started. And so that her eight circuits plus nineteen inches—or the consistent distance of her long throw—would not always come down from the upper groove at the same point on the circle, she had four different positions from which she could start the ball—at obstacles eight through eleven—and this shifting of her position, together with occasional uncontrolled short throws and "loopers," gave the proper look of variety.

Grebb could observe the point at which the throw began and know whether the throw was a medium or long and both of them were confident that, with so many known dependable factors, the pattern of play they'd need would emerge.

On a Wednesday night at midnight he came in to gather the final information they would need. He arrived with a bright-eyed gamin type—an "exotic dancer" from one of the clubs in Sparks, the next little town. He had a notebook and pencils and he bought fifty dollars' worth of quarter chips, giving his playmate a few stacks.

"My system tonight, blondie, or you like I should call you Ava?"

"Ava, if you please." She smiled impersonally and gave Cliff, who had drifted near, a private look of shared amusement.

"Well, then, Ava," he said importantly. "My system tonight is you tell me two numbers to play each time."

"I couldn't possibly," she began, looking at Cliff with a shrug.

"How come not? I don't ask you to guarantee anything. You just give me your favorite couple of numbers, or your hunch before each play and I'll play each of them."

The gamin said: "I'll give you hunches and we can split if you win."

"You play your stack, I'll play mine. How about it, Ava? I get these hunches sometimes and get me a run of luck and come out big." He looked over at Cliff. "The boss don't care. Hey, you don't care, do you, fella?"

"It's up to her."

"It might be fun," Ava said.

She set the ball spinning on a medium throw from Obstacle No. 9 and Grebb penciled M for "medium" and noted "9" as the starting position of the ball. The double zero at the moment her fingers let go of the ball was just past the chrome obstacle they had numbered "16."

Ava said: "My hunch is sixteen and two." He put the chip on "16" and "2" and wrote the information next to the "M" and the "9" on the first line of the notebook. He drew a dash and waited, watching the wheel, and in particular the point where the ball had come down from the upper groove. It passed its starting point, Obstacle 9, six times and went on seven more sixteenths of the circle and dropped out of the upper groove onto the obstacle-studded slope at almost exactly one inch beyond Obstacle No. 16.

Grebb saw and she saw, and neither of them spoke and when, without hitting any of the obstacles the ball finally settled in the "27" slot the gamin who had bet Odd and Red cried out: "I won both bets. Neither one of *her* hunches came through."

Grebb shrugged, wrote down "27" on the top line.

"So that's only the first play."

Ava paid the gamin's bets, took in Grebb's chips and started a spin from Obstacle 11—a long spin recorded on the second line of Grebb's notebook as "L . . . 11"—and she spotted the double zero at Obstacle 5, precisely opposite its center, and said aloud: "Five and zero."

Grebb recorded the information, and afterward the winning number. He played twenty times without a win. She threw a short ball and told him: "I can't think of anything." He made marks in the notebook and played his girl's hunch that time.

Before the night was over he had returned to play her four times, and he'd collected data on a hundred throws. The next night he was with a different girl and he got the data on another hundred plays. At various times during the next week he managed to compile a record on five hundred throws.

On her first night off she had a date with Cliff. Grebb came to her apartment the next evening and said: "I think I see the pattern, but I want a bigger sample. About two thousand plays. But I can't play your wheel that steadily without attracting suspicion. I'll come in with two people tonight. They'll take down information when I leave. I'll start the thing off by having you give me numbers, as usual. They'll catch on to the game and ask you to give *them* numbers. One of them you'll give the same information you've been giving me. He doesn't know anything except he thinks I'm superstitious about you. He can't observe the point from which you start your throw, and he won't know if it's a long or a medium. So the girl with him will get two other numbers from you. A medium throw will be any even number, 2-4-6 and so forth. Long will be any odd, 1-3-5, whatever you think of. Plus you'll give her the number of the obstacle, 8, 9, 10 or 11, from which you throw."

At first she listened attentively, leaning forward on the table. Then she slouched against the back of her chair, folded her arms across her chest. When he finished she tilted her head to one side, looked across at him speculatively.

"Are you out of your mind, Grebb?"

"What's wrong with it?"

"Everything. It's impossible. I've got all the load I can handle already without coding new people and plucking random numbers out of the air." She waved one hand, refolded her arms and shrugged. "I won't do it."

"Won't? You mean can't."

"I mean can't."

"That's better."

"I also mean won't," she said flatly. "And the 'won't' also applies to all future sex."

"Funny you should bring that up the moment I decided to have you."

"I mean it, Grebb."

"Of course," he said, amused. "In the future, no sex. After this time. Right?"

"Wrong. Nothing now," she said coolly. "Nothing ever."

"Lusting for your man right now, aren't you? Craving him! Want the rough feel of him. Have to have it the hard way, don't you?" he said in a low, warning voice. His left hand rolled on the table, the thumb outthrust in the direction of the sofa.

"No."

"Get in there!"

She remained slouched back on the chair.

There was an atmosphere about him that threatened constantly to spark into violence. It became visible now.

His bulging, amber eyes seemed on the point of bursting, his head jutted toward her, his thick shoulders hunched, his right hand, slack on the tabletop, clenched so tightly that the stretched skin over his knuckles shone slickly.

"Get off that chair or I'll knock you off it!"

Spots of color showed on the points of her cheeks. Her eyes widened involuntarily, her mouth felt dry. She breathed slowly, feeling the quickened drive of her pulse and sat still, defying him.

He got up so violently his chair crashed to the wall and toppled, hitting the floor loudly. He charged around the table. She remained slouched on the chair, arms folded.

"If I'm upset in any way," she said calmly, gazing directly at him, "my co-ordination will be gone. My control at the wheel will go to pieces."

He stood, fists clenched, glaring down at her.

"It's something to think about, isn't it?" she said with a soft insolence.

He relaxed, puffed his cheeks and blew out his breath. He turned, went over and picked up the chair, resettled himself across from her and sat scowling at her. She watched him, expressionless.

After a while he said gruffly: "You don't scare worth a damn any more, do you? I'm glad, you know that? You'll hold up all right during the actual big-money play. You won't fluster." He began to grin. "You're quite a doll. What would you say to us teaming up for a long run after we make our killing?"

"I've got my own plans."

"Such as."

"None of your business, Grebb."

"You think you've got the upper hand now?"

"I know it. In every department. You're soft on me. Most of the roughing up you've been giving me recently has been half-hearted—something you thought I wanted. I did. But I don't want it any more. I don't need it. And I don't need you. Everything at the wheel depends on me. I'm in the position where I could pick up anybody and set him down across from me and tell him what to do." She sat up straighter, her eyes snappish. She felt power surging in her.

"That's so, that's so," he agreed, nodding and grinning. "About me being soft on you, about everything depending on you, about your being able to boot me out of the scheme.

102

But let's be reasonable. I'm the one who's got the raw data on five hundred controlled plays. I've got it analyzed. Discovering the relationship between the known factors and the winning number is not a problem just anybody could figure. And if you're going to get too goddamned independent on me I'll just let you have the whole job to yourself. Only you'll have to collect new data. Or your stooge will do it for you, you think? He'll know how to use the known factors so he can predict where the ball slots?"

She shrugged. "I said I could pick up somebody; I didn't say I would. It wouldn't be reasonable."

"Here's the role of the guy on the other side of the table from you. He's got to take the information you give him and in a matter of seconds figure out what are the numbers to be bet. It's not as if you had one throw from one starting position and could arrive at a single formula and know once and for all that the sector where the ball would finally stop would be, say, nine or twenty or whatever number of slots to the left or the right of the double zero.

"No. You have two distinct throws and four starting points, and that's eight separate situations, each of them differently related to the double zero at the instant the play begins. How am I going to figure out within seconds the five-slot-wide sector in the wheel where the ball is most likely to drop and get my bets down? Well, I've got the sequence of numbers in the wheel memorized, and if you had one starting point, one speed of throw, I could make a rapid mental count—on your medium throw, for instance, from Obstacle Ten, the ball will, four times out of ten, finally settle in a five-slot-wide sector to the left of double zero. Four-five-six-seven-eight slots to the left, in fact—the actual numbers in the wheel being of course twenty-nine-twenty-two-eight-nineteen-thirty-one."

She blinked. "That's correct. You mean *four* times out of ten one of those numbers was hit—twenty-nine-twenty-two-eight-nineteen-thirty-one?"

He took an envelope out of his jacket. He shuffled through, brought out a sheet of paper. "Here's the story on your sixty-one medium throws from Obstacle Ten. One of those five numbers came up twenty-four times. Not quite four times out of ten."

"How did it work out on my other seven throws?" she asked urgently.

"This one was your best. But you didn't fall much under three times out of ten on any of them."

"May I look at the other records?"

He slipped out another sheet. "This one's your worst. Seventy longs from Obstacle Eleven and you averaged just under three out of ten—twenty hits. In this case the sector began eight slots to the right of double zero." He tossed her the envelope. "I'll get us coffee. Look them over. On the whole it's quite as good—well, Ava, even better than I'd hoped for."

She pored avidly over the figures on all eight sheets, scarcely noticing when he brought hot coffee for her, lit her cigarette. He sat, saying nothing, watching her smugly. She finally looked up at him.

"It's wonderful, Grebb. It's really working."

"You didn't believe it?"

She pushed nervously back at her hair. "I believed in it, but . . . well, I mean everything was so unco-ordinated— just pieces, not quite connected. But now, everything fits. It's real. It's going to happen and, Grebb, the sooner the better!"

"Five hundred plays isn't really enough."

"But my throws were as good as they'll ever be. The accuracy of my eye in spotting the double zero is as great as I can ever count on. I call it to the nearest inch, as well as I can judge, but I'll never be able to call it to the precise thousandth of an inch, and I couldn't communicate the information to you anyhow."

"That's the weakest link and nothing can be done. Something I failed to do till the last hundred plays was note the plays when the ball hit an obstacle. But when I began keeping track it was seven times on the hundred plays. That naturally messed up the pattern. On none of the plays where it hit an obstacle did we hit the five-slot win sector; so this actually raises your percentage. If only I could withdraw a bet when it hits an obstacle . . . but that would look too fishy. Now, if you could hold on, give me time to memorize what I'll have to know about all eight of your throws . . ."

"Couldn't you write it down? Refer to it?"

"Yes. That wouldn't be hard. In fact, I've been thinking of masking our play by having some numerology-astrology books. . . . I could hide my reference table in one of them.

104

. . . Next week I'll pop in and we'll play for money and win a few thousand."

"Next week a *few* thousand? Listen, I can't wait. The crowds since the Memorial Day weekend have been driving me to distraction. It's a strain, Grebb. I want to push this, speed it up. I thought you had backing, I thought you could get the stake for big-money play right away. If I have to stand around earning it a few hundred or thousand at a time—well, I just don't have the time.

"Cliff wants to put an engagement ring on me, he wants me to come to Sunday dinners with his damned family every week. He hangs on me, he moons over me, he wants to set a wedding date. I can't play the love side of this game much longer. If I have to go through with any more of that, I give up. What are you, a fake? You said you had big-bankroll people behind you."

He shook his head nervously, put a finger to his lips. "Keep your voice down. In the first place, I told you this deal is mine, mine alone—you and me. If the syndicate got word of me knocking off on them . . ." He aimed a fore-finger, jerked his thumb in a silent gun-like gesture. "I've got a few thousand ready money but I've got to account for every nickel."

"When you run out on them, what difference does it make?"

"None. But how's a mug like me going to account for thousands of dollars without the casino smelling a rat?"

"You won it, for God's sake, you won it! Come in blowing off with your big loud mouth and flash it around and tell the world you won it at the Mapes or someplace, and you won it with your numerology and astrology books and the stars and numbers are right for you and you could ask the day and hour and minute of my birth and insist that I am astrologically and numerologically right for your luck.

"You've been figuring to play during one of the big conventions when there was big money play so you wouldn't be noticed, but there's no way to be sure there'd by any real big-money play. They still laugh about the oilmen's convention a few years ago when all those millionaires were buying dime chips. Anyway, you've been on the scene too long not to be noticed. That astrology-numerology gag is good, and right in keeping with a hunch nut like you

105

make yourself out. Let's hit them now—tomorrow night when I go back to work."

"I'd have to go to S.F. and pick up more cash. I can give them a story and get it."

"You come in. Flash your money and ask for big action because you're hot and your charts tell you to hit the wheel. Tomorrow night!"

"Sure. Hell, yes. Why not now?"

"We'll stand there and we'll slaughter them. If I could hit the first four times at a thousand-dollar bet each time, a hundred and forty thousand! They'd faint and close the wheel. I'd be so upset I'd have to get out. And that's the last they'd see of me. I'd be on my way!" Her eyes gleamed.

Eleven

When Grebb was gone Ava looked around the little apartment with the same sense of remoteness from it she had felt when she first moved in because she was now, in all but the physical sense, already gone from it and entered into another phase. She began to gather her personal belongings, her books, and packets of letters and snapshot albums, stacks of unplayed piano music, her dresses and her underclothing and records and little radio and record player and insurance policies and shoes and stockings and she carried them in leisurely trips out to her car beginning at midnight and she was almost done at two A.M. She stood looking into the closet at some of her winter things and then she shrugged and left them there because winter was an unimaginable distance away.

She showered, smiling down at the slick, baby-pink-and-white fatness of her belly sticking out down there with a sort of delightful impudence. She fastidiously made herself pleasing to her own senses from head to toe and dressed herself in a fresh and summery lavender and white cotton dress and white pumps.

The waist of the dress was high, the skirt airy and full in order to conceal, as did a girdle when she was in her casino uniform, that secret zone. The slenderness of her figure made the contained area of fatness improbable and unnoticed by the casual eye. But her very slenderness made the bulge pronounced and surely obvious to the intimate lingerings of Cliff's hands. There were no lingerings or close inspections about Grebb's intimacies, but even he couldn't have failed to notice.

Incredibly, neither gave any evidence of suspicion, each had absolute confidence that he knew her; it was surely a tribute to her total success in mastering deceit.

She strolled out to her car, free and gone, within twenty-four hours of departure on the final journey, thinking of the hours ahead as marking time, like someone in a depot playing cards till train or plane time, and there was a certain pleasant, uninvolved flavor about the farewell, an almost affectionate mood toward this setting which had been connected with this long, long intermission, this pre-emergent time of her life.

She parked on the perimeter of the downtown area and walked the several blocks into the brightly lighted, super-crowded casino area where streets and walks and alleys and the lighted buildings teemed with a pageantry of unreal people, and she went into the noisy, bright, surging remoteness of the Fourleaf Club, because Cliff was on duty tonight and while she was still physically marking time she must remain in the proper role.

She had a meal with him and then she walked back out of the crowds toward her car and a car filled with hoodlums roared past and they shouted at her and it came racing back and slowed and they were drunk or drugged and rapish in mood and she smiled and moved on with a blissful sense of immunity and when a touring police car sent the hoodlums racing off she was not even relieved since she was no longer afraid, really, of anything.

She got into her car and took a main highway out of town, indifferent to the race and rush of other cars sweeping past, darting hell-bent from the motels, all of it a wildness and feverishness of the moment and she followed an old familiar zigzag of roads onto secondary and untraveled roads and found a vast patch of empty desert, studded at this season with flowering plants of every variety, gray now in the starlight, but scenting the air. She got out of the car.

How sweet the night, the warmth of dry air, the distant summer snow, dim as cloud, on mountain peaks! There was above her a depth and purity and profound blackness of space and the stars in their bejeweled, galactic splendor were tiny, spinning multicolored points of light. She felt the stirring of the other life in her and of her own spirit's new freedom and she knew the joy of the first life emerging from the elemental slime, unknowing yet driven to fulfill that which had been written. . . .

He had come to her in the night, her one mate, her lover and her deity, he had come to her—she remembered it clearly and for the first time—yes, he had spent the honeymoon in California, but he had known she was here and he had come away from the mate prescribed for him by other forces and he had waked her from her sleep and kissed her lips and stroked her cheeks and the biological necessity in him had asserted itself and he had penetrated her nakedly and her womb had opened and taken his seed and now . . . now . . .

She caressed her belly, a total sweetness and sense of beauty filling her, and she wept without pain and faced the horror that lay at the end of the final journey without recoiling from it—*because the seed grown in the belly of his untrue mate must be destroyed . . . and the carrier of that seed must die . . . and Dave himself must die*—and her hate was clean and clear to her and there was the strength in her to bear it and to be truly the scourge of God.

She stared into the night and vowed with a slow and solemn dedication to strike back in vengeance, to destroy him who had destroyed her and beside him in his final agony would lie his woman and his child. . . .

Ava was smiling and prettily flushed with a contained excitement when she drove back to her apartment.

During the day she made a trip to town to have her car serviced and to close out four hundred dollars in her checking account, then she slept on and off all day, dreaming little, feeling no tiredness or tension when she woke.

Cliff phoned at seven, wanting to drop by, but she made excuses and almost as he hung up Grebb called.

"I got it," he said.

"The money?"

"Yes. Not as much as I wanted. But it'll have to do."

"You'd better come over."

"The Hamilton character won't be popping in?"

"No."

Grebb seemed almost to resent her calm when he came in.

"Frankly," he said, "I'm tense. I want to go over just exactly how we'll operate, then how we'll get out of town. I think it would be better to use your car."

"No."

"Just for a while. You see, there was a little trouble getting the money. I don't know if I convinced them. I had to tell them a tale about paying off some hoods; I half-got the impression that they didn't wholly go for it. They put it out because they're sure I wouldn't dare mess around with them. On the other hand, they may be tailing me—they know my car, naturally—so we've got to use yours. Park at the Sky Garage and I'll pick you up there. If anybody's tailing me, I'll have them shaken by then and we can be on the road before they have any idea where I went."

For the next hour they sat across from each other at the dinette table while he talked and talked, going over what they would be doing. She listened only vaguely, and looked at him with a curiously emotionless objectivity, thinking he had served her well, had truly made it possible for her to gain the tough honesty to face the always-repressed, dark side of her feelings toward Dave.

Perhaps, she speculated idly, she should never have idealized Dave and romanticized her own love as if it had existed without hostility. On the other hand, had she been capable of doing that, the darkness wouldn't have grown to true power and she would not have this new and exultant experience to look forward to. She shifted on her chair, and Grebb smiled.

"I'm glad to see you showing a little enthusiasm!" he stated. "For a while there you were too cool to be true. I want you cool and calm and in absolute control, but not with that attitude."

"What attitude?" She frowned in surprise.

"That nasty look, like you held a grudge. Listen, Ava. You can't mess *me* up tonight without messing yourself up. Keep your mind on that. You want the money as much as I do."

"Of course," she assured him. "The nasty look was at myself—a back look at myself. I *was* a loony when we met. Out of my mind. No more. I give you credit, Grebb. You

109

yanked me out of it. I was on the point of killing the wrong person."

"Killing the wrong person?"

"Me." She laughed quietly. Her eyes were fever-bright and strange to watch. "I really almost killed myself just before you came along. It's amazing, when I look back at what I was, to think I could have let myself be so soft." She shrugged, the lovely line of her lips hardening and stiffening. "So I'll park in the Sky Garage. My car's not much, but it'll hold together. And the first overnight stop we make, we separate. No sharing motels or anything like that. Understood?"

"Sure, sure, but how about reconsidering what you said last night? Just this once. I'm too tense. I need a relaxer. Let's have a party now." He looked at his watch. "Plenty of time."

Ava got up, strolled over to the sink, opened a drawer. When she turned around she was holding a butcher knife. She returned to the table, sat down calmly, the knife on her lap.

Grebb blinked. "Hell, all you had to say was 'no.' At a time like this I'm sure not going to *rape* you."

"I know you're not."' She smiled at him, a gesture of the lips while the eyes remained wickedly cool and intent.

"What do you want to get vicious for when you know I'm a little soft on you?"

"Maybe that's why. Get unsoft. Keep believable. Remember it's hate that makes the world go 'round." She laughed derisively.

At the sound of the doorbell Grebb's eyes flicked left, recentered, and his heavy eyebrows lifted. Ava shrugged and Grebb was suddenly on his feet, in a semi-crouch, his legs spanning the chair. He lifted the chair back silently so it didn't scrape and headed diagonally for the bathroom and entered. Ava pushed back her chair, carried the knife and the ash tray they'd been using to the sink. She emptied the ashtray and put the knife in the drawer.

Peering at herself in the thermometer-edged little square mirror on the wall over the sink, she felt relaxed but the upper curves of her eyelids seemed shallow as if drawn tensely.

She relaxed into wide-eyed innocence and walked to the door and opened the peephole, as careful of her precious self as her protector Cliff had cautioned her to be and

110

scuffed metal on metal as if opening the chain lock which hung loose.

"Cliff!" she cried in a gay voice loud enough for Grebb to hear as she swung the door wide.

Ordinarily the sight of her smile would have made his own waiting smile leap with life and the young, eager lines of his face fatten and lift, crinkling his eyes.

Now he stood limply in a pair of clean but very old saggy-kneed white duck pants and a blue-green-silver sports shirt which only emphasized the long gloom of his face. His eyes pleaded with her silently and she knew with a sudden, terrible, twisting sensation in her breast and a brief locking of her throat muscles that he knew something which hurt him.

Her own smile faded and as he came in he looked at her and tried to smile and he suddenly looked away and drew in his breath. She knew exactly that need to draw breath, to fill an emptiness, to banish the terrible heaviness that could not be banished—for it was the symptom of a loss, of a loss of love, of a loved one, a feeling indescribable and unmistakable and known deeply to her. Her arms reached out to comfort him but they were ghost arms because her own hung motionless.

"What's wrong, Cliff?" she said.

"He's here, isn't he? His car's here again. It's true, isn't it? I wouldn't believe it, but it's true, isn't it?" He couldn't look at her, and his voice held a tragic note of misery.

"You're here, only you," she said.

"You've been seeing him, haven't you?" he said, then hurried on. "Please, don't lie to me, Ava. How long has it been going on?"

Ava gazed deeply into his eyes, feeling for a moment a bond of pain and sympathy with him so acute that she wanted to spare him. Their voices were low and Grebb couldn't have heard. She could send Cliff on his way without trouble. A lovely notion. She turned and walked slowly to the bathroom and opened the door, and said sharply to Grebb: "Get him!"

Grebb charged across the room at him, his head turtled between his hunched shoulders. Cliff, momentarily startled, sidestepped and brought up his arms and aimed a wide-flying roundhouse blow.

Grebb sprang sideward, his shoulder striking Cliff's chest and bumping him off balance. In the next instant Grebb turned and began to pile blows into Cliff's body—hard, thudding punches so fast Ava couldn't count them, while Cliff flailed at Grebb's sides with ineffectual blows.

Grebb's knee jerked up sharply. Cliff grunted and tried to back off but Grebb crowded him, battering relentlessly at his body and head until he had him against the wall, when he suddenly smashed a fist full into Cliff's throat. As Cliff made a cawing-coughing sound and tried to twist around and shield himself, Grebb flattened him against the wall again and smashed lightning rights and lefts into Cliff's stomach below the belt. Grebb jumped backward, then, doubling forward, he hurled his whole weight forward, butting like a goat. Cliff's legs collapsed under him and he slipped to the floor. Grebb whirled and spoke tersely to Ava.

"Help me get him up and out to my car."

Grebb, sweating, bent down and hooked an arm around Cliff's waist and Ava on the other side supported his limp, unconscious body.

"Hey," Grebb ordered sharply, "wake up and walk! C'mon, c'mon, help carry yourself, you bastard."

Cliff remained semiconscious, enough to help them walk him out and along the walk and to Grebb's station wagon. Driving out to the edge of town and studying the streets and vacant lots, Grebb said tersely, "I didn't want to leave him in your place. Here's a good spot. I'll finish him off here."

Stumbling through the empty lot between them, Cliff jerked and mumbled something and Grebb turned and faced him. Bracing his feet apart and holding both hands together he brought them up in a violent heaving motion that caught Cliff under the chin with such force that he did a back dive, his head striking hard ground.

Grebb walked to him unhurriedly and, seizing Cliff's hair, he pounded his head on the ground a dozen times, then stood up and kicked him in the face with the point of one shoe and then the other. He stepped closer and smashed down with the heel of his shoe, then he stepped on Cliff's chest and leaped into the air, drawing his knees and feet upward and came down, striking with both feet close together like a single, enormous fist driven by the powerful muscles of his legs and the weight of his body.

There was a crunching as of cracked ribs and Grebb leaped again on Cliff's chest and then his stomach. Then he caught one of Cliff's arms and levered the unconscious body over onto its stomach and stomped his back several times. He got off and kicked his head once or twice with lessened force and then stood quiet, panting a little.

"Quit looking and upsetting yourself," Grebb told Ava, who had been standing motionless, mute, stricken, staring at the helpless, battered, unconscious body, dark with gore there on the dark ground.

"He's not moving," she whispered hoarsely.

Grebb squatted beside Cliff for a long time. He stood up. "He's alive." Grebb started for the car.

"Where are you going?" Ava hissed.

"C'mon! We've got to get away from here!"

She wet her dry lips: "You're not going to—" she said hoarsely—"finish?" He seized her arm, yanked her forward.

"I'm done! Plenty of time for us to be on our way."

Riding on the far side of the seat from him and staring out the window, she was vaguely aware of Grebb worrying aloud that she might be too upset, that her control might be gone.

"That's a laugh," she said, the odd brightness still in her eyes. "I never felt better in my life."

Twelve

Ava tipped the car jockey at the Sky Garage a silver dollar to hold her car on the lower floor for quick pickup and started toward the Fourleaf and her final session on duty at the wheel. Visitors packed the gaudy, noisy center of town. The alleys which ran behind or intersected the big casinos were flowing and counterflowing and eddying with cross currents of people. Shops and restaurants as well as the gambling places were open and there was a carnival-rodeo atmosphere to the place. As she moved unhurriedly along avoiding all contacts, a two-man city patrol car came along at a silent creep and one of the officers winked and wagged a lazy hand out his side window, and spoke to her in passing.

She thought nothing of it when she saw Fred Carson,

the balding, round-faced, oval-bodied general manager of the Fourleaf Club standing outside and looking in her direction. He often stepped out in the summer to "favor his lung with unconditioned air." He was so laughably without emotion that the girls privately dubbed him Mr. Personality or Mr. Passion.

"Hello, Ava."

"Hello, Mr. Carson. The outside air is nice tonight."

"I wonder if you'd come down to the office."

"Now or after I change into uniform?"

"I think now. I asked Mr. Fritz to come in. We'd like your opinion on a matter."

They went into the Fourleaf.

Her circling gaze touched Grebb for a split second as she and Mr. Carson reached the basement steps. Without seeming to have noticed, Mr. Carson observed: "You know that fellow." It wasn't a question—nor an accusation either.

"That one? Oh, yes, he's in often. I was looking for Cliff."

"So are we," Mr. Carson said, as they went down the steps.

"He's not in yet?"

Whether or not he heard her against the din of the play at the basement games, Mr. Carson didn't answer, and his expression was neutral. But he was walking at her side even though the stairway was crowded and she had the feeling that his lateral vision was quite good and that he was observing her expression.

When they reached the lower floor she dropped behind him, reasonably enough, she assured herself, because the aisle between the games and the lunch counters wasn't wide. He wouldn't suspect it was a move to avoid scrutiny, not unless he already knew something, not unless Cliff had been found and had regained consciousness.

There was a momentary blurring of her vision and the necessity in her to draw breath and she remembered the moment when she had felt the bond with Cliff and might have turned back and it was eerily interesting that that feeling of emptiness-heaviness in the chest, the feeling requiring the intake of breath, was not alone connected with the loss of love but with fear and it might not be so eerie a connection but one and the same thing—fear, loss of love —fear, need of breath.

Mr. Carson opened the *Employees Only* entrance door and held it for her to precede him down the narrow, quiet

114

hall. He caught up with her at the end of it and opened the door into the office for her. She stepped across the threshold, her eyes closing for just a moment against the sudden sure knowledge and terror that he would be standing there; gory and half-dead and risen to accuse and damn her. She opened her eyes and it was only Mr. Fritz, one of the chief owners and very seldom on the scene.

A narrow, intense little man with graying, thick black hair, he was dressed, now as always, in defiance of the local customs in a dark blue business suit and tie. He was on his feet, peering at her, his eyes squinting slightly behind black horn-rims, the expression on his face a pinched, total disapproval. It was his normal expression; his greeting was friendly.

"Evening, Ava. Fred's telling me about a fellow he says you know—"

"Not personally," Mr. Carson put in blandly.

"Of course. His name's something like Gat—"

"Grebb," Ava said.

"Yes. Grebb. Do you think he's been reading your arm?"

She frowned, dropped her gaze, opened her purse. "I don't think so." She got out cigarettes, put one to her lips.

Mr. Fritz stepped instantly forward, catching up the desk lighter. He held the flame for her, peering at her with that meaningless look of disapproval.

"Cliff's warned me about that many times, Mr. Fritz, and—" she smiled, nodded at Mr. Carson—"Mr. Carson has mentioned it. That Grebb is the sort of man I'd immediately," she broke off, clamped her upper arms against her sides as if containing a shudder, "immediately mistrust and recoil from. You know."

Mr. Fritz stood close, watching her, nodding eagerly. "I know. I know. Mr. Carson pointed him out." He smiled at her, sobered again instantly as if he'd long known how unattractive his smile was. "He would naturally clash with a girl of your caliber."

"What concerned us was his numerous appearances at your wheel when he was asking you for numbers," Mr. Carson said smoothly.

She smiled wryly. "He's a hunch nut. One time it's one thing, one time it's another. He'll suddenly bolt away from the wheel and rush to the craps table, or go to another wheel."

"You don't think he's keeping track of the winning

115

numbers—it's reported that he was keeping a book, as if developing a system—you don't think, then, that he has been able to make anything out of your particular style of throw?"

She laughed. "There's just no way he could, because I never throw the same way twice. I move around, start the ball from one place and another and vary my speeds and deliberately guard against just that problem of anyone reading my arm. I'm alert against the danger of falling into a routine. No, I don't think he could possibly have any sort of an edge. Mainly, he doesn't have the patience."

"And the ones who do," Mr. Fritz said, looking at Mr. Carson, "they sit and write down numbers in their little books for thousands of plays without betting a dime—work in teams, in shifts around the clock." He guffawed, a harsh metallic sound. "Then they put down their money and two days later they're borrowing bus fare home from us."

Both men laughed together.

"Will that be all?" Ava said, "I'd better get into uniform. And I want to make a phone call. I can't understand where Cliff is,"

"Her fiancé," Mr. Carson told Mr. Fritz.

"I know. . . . I know. . ." They both beamed at her. "He'll be here. Cliff's regular; don't you worry a minute about that boy. He probably had car trouble someplace up in the hills. . . . But now the reason for this special request for your opinion is that this Gat—I mean Grebb—wants to play five-hundred-dollar chips."

"No!" Ava stared at them solemnly. She burst out laughing. "One five-hundred-dollar - chip? I'm sure he couldn't buy more. He's the biggest braggart I ever heard. Cliff and I laugh at him all the time. He's always blowing off about how much he won in Vegas or Carson or Virginia City or Tahoe—always someplace else he was the big-shot, big-stakes gambler. In the next breath he'll throw out two silver dollars and say: 'Gimme a stack!' Dime chips. When he puts down real money would be the time to worry about him—which'll be never."

"This time he said he won it in Vegas, and he showed real money. He's got a book on the stars and a couple on numerology. He's sure this is his night and you're his croupier and he wants to play. So I think we'll just let him. We can use his seven, eight thousand."

When she came down from the women employees'

116

lounge in uniform ready for work two guards had to wedge her through the tightly packed crowd. Most of the other play on the main floor had stopped, and news of Grebb had wild-fired up and down the street and people were surging in from other casinos. The table was cleared of other players and Grebb sat there with fifteen gold-plated five-hundred-dollar chips, and a stack of silver dollars. He was flipping pages and scowling at the pages of his booklets on numerology and astrology.

He'd wanted to play for thousand-dollar chips and have enough for five plays but he hadn't got the money and they figured on her percentage of accuracy holding up so that one of the three plays he had the money for would hit and finance the rest.

He looked up with a shout of enthusiasm.

"There you are. Hi, Ava! I'm out for bear tonight. All the charts and tables are right and I'm coming up with a half-million-dollar win. I got it made, a combo of two sciences, astrology and numerology. No more hunches for me. You figure just right for my luck. The day and hour and minute you were born is right in line with my personal number groupings for this day."

"Imagine!" Ava said mockingly. "Such scientific preparation. Now that I think back on it, I noticed you there in the hospital making notes when I was born. You were younger then, that's probably why I didn't recognize you."

He laughed with the crowd. "She's a bright chick, this one." He smiled then with a calculated look of idiotic slyness. "Only, the fact is I got you to tell me the day and hour and minute yourself, you and Marissa here both. I leave it to her if I didn't, just casual like, last week. So I *do* know your stars and the rundown on your astrology charts is accurate right to the minute," he said triumphantly. He looked to the left and to the right and nodded with mild gloating and enormous self-satisfaction. "Sciences, especially two of them combined together, are still better than mere hunches. So you better string along with me tonight instead of your own hunches."

"You didn't win with my hunches last week?" she said distractedly, looking at the wheel. She dipped a hand languorously and gave the wheel a few pushes, boosting its speed and gave Fred Carson a brief, meaningful glance. She had warned Grebb that she might have to do this, to reassure whoever was observing the play. Carson believed in varying not only the throws but the speed of the wheel.

"I broke about even on your hunches, and I got nothing against them in the slightest, Ava. If you want, we'll go ahead and play your hunches."

Ava laughed with a note of condescension. "A minute ago you had a scientific system."

There was laughter and tittering from the crowd, and Marissa Lopez, beside Ava, had to suck her cheeks to keep from laughing in his face. Meantime the wheel, finely balanced for stability, was settling back to what Grebb called the cruising speed natural to it, which would hold steadily for fifteen seconds before any perceptible deceleration set in.

Grebb, annoyed at seeming ridiculous, blustered: "I still got a scientific system. I never meant I wasn't going to use it for *me*. What I meant was to do you a favor and make side bets for you also, in addition to making my own bets." He lifted a few of the top coins in the stack of silver dollars, let them drop jinglingly back. "These I was going to bet for you, with me or against me, like a sport."

"Don't do me any favors. I don't want you to bet for me, with you or with my own hunches." She plucked the ball riding in one of the slots, peering at it, rolling it in her fingers. She took the spare ball, inspected it, her eyes and mouth sulky. "Are you ready to bet?"

"You're sore. Don't jinx me, Ava. Leave me bet for you. Say you ain't sore and won't jinx me."

She gave him an exasperated look. "I'm not sore. I'll be glad to have you bet for me. It's very nice of you. Shall we get on with it?"

"Ready. Let's go. And," he said, frowning at Marissa and Fred Carson and Mr. Fritz there behind the wheel with her, "don't nobody try to jinx me, touching the ball or wheel or anything to jinx me."

She shifted into position to throw from Obstacle No. 10, her most accurate. Grebb observed it and he would recognize her medium throw and her two "hunch numbers" spoken aloud would give him to the nearest inch the position of the "00" at the instant the ball left her fingers. He would consult his table of variables, concealed there in one of the astrology books, and be able to determine the distance, left or right of "00," to the five-slot-wide sector where the ball would settle three times out of ten or four

118

times out of ten or, more to the immediate point, once out of three times.

When she took the ball, ready to begin the play, everyone in the front rows of the crowds ringing the wheel became quiet and intently watchful, and those behind them sensed that the play was beginning and the hush rolled back over them. Nearer at hand she could feel the nervousness of Mr. Fritz. She sensed the neutral expression of Fred Carson as a mask. She wondered if Grebb had overplayed, if his true cunning didn't show through as clearly as markings on a crooked deck to these fraud-alert eyes.

She had started the ball on its spin and spoken her "hunch numbers" aloud and Grebb had placed silver-dollar bets and begun to scowl at the table of variables and the ball had circled three times and then four and four and a half and he had not yet made his computations. She saw a small sheen of sweat on his forehead as if the pressure of time squeezed his skull and she waited coolly, watching the ball and it came down from the upper groove and his bet wasn't made yet and she thought indifferently that it would be his failure, not hers, because she could stand there under the tense pressure of the crowd and the nearby guards and the management and, superior to their outer threat and her own inner anxieties, function like a splendid machine, neither hating nor loving nor fearing nor feeling.

He began to make his bet, placing the five chips in a scatter pattern up and down the layout, though the numbers were side by side in the wheel. The ball was on the slope, its circuiting and rate of descent down toward the wheel even, and it sliced a clean diagonal between a vertical and a horizontal chrome obstacle, missing both, and hovered closer and closer to the edge of the wheel like a white hawk surveying the numbers rushing toward it, choosing one to pounce on. Finally, the ball dropped with a single, firm *tick* of sound and didn't bounce out of the slot, and even before she realized it someone in the crowd shouted, spotting the win.

She smiled wryly and raked in her two silver dollars and four of his gold-plated chips and measured out a short and a long stack of chips as if they were worth thirty-five dimes instead of thirty-five five-hundred-dollar chips. Seventeen thousand five hundred, minus four losing chips made the play worth fifteen thousand five hundred to them —correction—fifteen thousand four hundred ninety-eight.

119

Grebb raked in the chips smiling to himself. He prepared for his next bet, lining up five two-chip stacks.

"Raising your unit to one thousand dollars?" Mr Fritz said.

"Too much? Want me to back off?" Grebb guffawed. "At five hundred dollars a unit it'll just take me longer. How do you want it, slow torture or get the misery over faster?"

"I don't think you'll break us. Bet what you want."

Ava started a new play and he got down her two bets and then a bleakness flattened his features and his hands fumbled as he started to consult his books. Just before the ball slotted he gave a sickly grin and threw up his hands.

"It wasn't right. The numbers didn't tell me nothing."

"Maybe," Mr. Fritz said, smiling unpleasantly, "you'd like to quit while you're ahead."

"Just you get down to the safe and check up if you've got the ready to make good."

"The Fourleaf Club," he assured Grebb and the crowd, "never welched on a bet."

Ava was coolly paying off a win on one of the silver dollar bets. "You had something going for you, at least," she said. "*My* hunches."

"It's yours, it's yours. . . . Rake it in and stick it in your pocket with my compliments. Now, let's play some roulette!"

He wiped sweat from his face, lit a cigarette, then noticed he had a new-lit cigarette in another ash tray. He laughed at himself, but he had paled slightly; at the time she thought he'd been shaken by his failure to make the computations quickly enough.

Next play he made the calculations on time and made five thousand-dollar bets and lost. Fred Carson's mouth went up a fraction of an inch. Grebb played and lost again and she didn't know whether it was a mistake in his figuring or merely that the system was calculated to lose six times out of ten and still win. She had no doubts whatever about the accuracy of her throw or her eye because the pressure hadn't touched her, she'd never functioned better.

He lost another five thousand.

And another.

He got down another five-thousand-dollar bet and she knew without herself making a chip count that Fred Carson saw with relief that Grebb couldn't make another full play, would have to cut back his bets, and a couple of losses would wipe him out. The mood in the casino was restless; she could tell from the tone of the constant voice murmur that the crowd was against the house, was being beaten with Grebb, that however damn-foolish they knew his system to be they shared an underlying belief in irrational Lady Luck. Suddenly a cheer began like a burst of firecrackers around the front rows, quickly chain-reacting through the whole casino.

She paid out thirty-five thousand dollars.

He lost five.

She paid him thirty-five thousand more. The voice drone of the crowd was distant in her ears and she looked at Grebb's shirt and knew he had changed it because Cliff's blood had spattered him.

The body heat of the excited crowd rose against the cooling system and gave the air a clamminess that made the sweat crawl on her scalp, and ooze under her blouse and under her girdle and Grebb was a stranger, his eyes bulging and remote and she knew she must break his and her run of luck, end this vile partnership. She would not speak the numbers he needed and her throw must become erratic.

She tried to disrupt the machine-like accuracy of her arm and her eye. Then she was speaking aloud the "hunch numbers" and her throw ended with another win, and there was nothing, nothing she could do except move along the prescribed pattern which had taken her over completely. . . .

Grebb was standing up. The play was finished. Triumph was arrogantly clear on his face.

"I can't stand this," Ava said, "I can't stand any more. I've got to get out of here."

"Don't worry—don't worry, it wasn't your fault. . . ." Somebody comforted her. As she left the wheel the crowd seemed to part for her. They looked at her with a kind of awe and she knew she must look shockingly disturbed and she covered her face, and under her hands her cheeks spread and a sobbing came out of her throat sounding exactly like laughter.

"I'll be all right. . . . I'll be all right," she said, outside. "I just need fresh air, Mr. Carson. Don't worry about me."

121

Grebb came running, shouting: "Ava . . . Ava." He pushed several bills into her hand. "A tip! A one-grand tip." He hurried back into the club.

She was walking away. Free. Uncaught. Uncaught and happy, a thousand dollars in one fist, thirty-six silver dollars in her pocket thumping against her leg with every stride and there was more money in her billfold and her car was waiting and ready and she could change clothes somewhere a thousand or a hundred miles away and if he got it all in cash it would be fifty-four thousand for her and that much for him and then she was in her car, and in the Sky Garage, waiting through one cigarette and two cigarettes and of course it would take time to get the money.

And there he came. Walking fast. Flicking glances behind him. She had the car started when he got in.

"Head over for Sparks, then we'll go up toward Pyramid Lake. I've got some things in a motel up there—the Desert Ship Motel."

"I know where it is," she said, watching the street as she headed out of the garage. "You got the money?"

He was peering at the back window. He glanced at her, patted his waist. "Right here. Money belt. All cash. We'll split at the motel. Step on it. Let's get out of here."

He peered at the back window for a few more minutes. "What're you looking for?"

He straightened in the seat, switched on the radio.

"I can't tell a damned thing. A dozen cars, probably none of them following us. You know that second play? I couldn't get my bet down? I saw one of the trigger boys." He was silent for a while. "I was afraid they were suspicious of the tale I had to give them to get the stake. Maybe they were. Or maybe the trigger was just hanging around."

"It doesn't prove anything, your winning the money," Ava pointed out. "You might have planned to turn it in to the syndicate."

They were going through Sparks.

"There's the turn that'll take us out to my motel."

She pulled up at the intersection, waited, cut left in the general direction of Pyramid Lake. Grebb fooled with the radio dial, getting a mishmash of musical fragments.

"No goddamned news!"

"There will be," she calmed him. "They didn't know about Cliff at the casino when I came on duty. I mentioned him. If they'd had word, if he'd been found, if he'd regained consciousness and talked, we'd never have made the killing."

"I guess," he said, his attention elsewhere.

He was twisted sideways watching through the back window. There were several cars on the same road. "If I was being watched by that trigger, it's not good. If he just happened to be on the scene and didn't know this was my private play, it's okay. He'll report what he saw, but by then we'll have a full day's start. But my winning the money will prove plenty to the bosses. I'd have discussed any move like this with them. They have to okay every move I make. This *couldn't* be just something I forgot to tell them about. Anyway I've got a gun at the motel."

"A gun?"

"A blaster. A beauty. A flat, sweet, blue-steel beauty. An automatic. An eight-shooter. I'll feel better with a trigger of my own."

"They know about me," Ava said. "They know about me, now that I'm with you. And if they're out after you with guns, they're out after me, too."

"Smart deduction."

She looked sharply toward him, at the road, at him again. "You're glad they know about me, too, aren't you?"

"Hell, no. If I thought they knew about you and recognized your car, I'd be in the soup for sure."

"You keep looking for someone following us."

"You never know. Maybe they've been tailing me a long time. Like that Hamilton character, he knew about me and you. Maybe the boys in Frisco know more than I thought."

The yellow and red Desert Ship Motel sign glowed a mile or so ahead.

"If they know about you they'll know where you live and they'll come right here, maybe they're here aready. I'm not going to stop at that motel. Maybe we should cut back, not even pass it."

"I don't live there. I live where I told you, the Norwalt Hotel. If there's a squad out instead of just one trigger, one will wait at the Norwalt, one of them at my car. Nobody at the Desert Ship. They don't know about it."

"You think. You hope."

"I think. I hope."

"I won't stop," she said. She added in a strangely calm voice, "It's not time for me to die."

123

"Hell, it's not going to come to anybody dying. At worst they'll hijack us. Grab the money. That's all they'd be after."

"If you get a gun and they've got guns—"

"Shut up, Ava. You held up fine. Your control was beautiful. This is no time to get hysterical."

"If they were there, I don't know what they'd do to me, and you don't either. I want to keep going. I've got to go on, I've got things to do. Nothing must stop me."

The motel, its forty or fifty cabins spread over several acres, was within a quarter-mile.

"Just slow down and we'll cruise past. I can see from the road if there's a car around my cabin, if they're waiting."

"If we slow and they see us . . ."

"We won't stop, just slow down. I've got a suitcase with important things in it."

"And a gun."

"Yes. But forget that. Nothing will happen to *you*. Me they could be sore at and they'd be in the mood to put me in the hospital for a few months," he laughed humorlessly, "maybe in the bed next to the Hamilton character. But what would they have against you? Nothing whatsoever. As far as you knew it was no skin off of them. They wouldn't hurt you; I'd clear you with them. So slow down."

She dropped their speed. Passing the motel she peered with him though she had no idea where, exactly, he was looking.

"I think it's all right," Grebb said hesitantly. He cleared his throat. "Go back."

She nipped her underlip, glanced at the rear-view mirror and cut onto the shoulder. She U-turned and drove back to the neon-lighted entranceway.

"Slow down at the office."

She slowed while Grebb pushed his face into the window opening and waved. The on-duty man in the little office smiled and nodded and Ava accelerated, peering at the directional signs at the fork of the road ahead.

"Turn left. Number 17. The fourth cabin."

Infrequent dots of overhead lights along the roadways together with the glow through the shut blinds of a dozen cabins illuminated the grounds weakly. The third cabin was dark, as was No. 17, and the neighboring cabin twenty yards beyond. All three carports were empty. She started to turn into the port of No. 17.

"No," Grebb said, opening his door, and dangling a key case. "I'll get my stuff. You drive to the next intersection, turn around and come back."

She nodded. He left the car and moved swiftly to the cabin. She drove ahead to the intersection about two hundred yards away. When she turned and started back, focusing on Grebb's cabin, she saw he hadn't yet turned on the lights. She stopped in front of the cabin. The door was open. She got out a cigarette, depressed the dashboard lighter, staring at the empty, open doorway. She lit the cigarette, and revved the car engine loudly two or three times. She let the motor idle, realized her neck was tense, her head tilted to listen. There were driftings of partyish sounds from a cabin somewhere, but no light or movement within No. 17.

Why was he trying to find things in the dark when they were in a rush to get away? The why was obvious. He hadn't been sure it was safe to come back here; he didn't know if they knew about this cabin or not. She squirmed on the seat, blinking rapidly, wondering suddenly if they'd been laying for him in there and he was dead. . . . A figure appeared in the doorway and she became rigid.

An instant later she knew it was Grebb and relaxed. He set down his suitcase to close the door, so she knew he must have something in his other hand. When he moved nearer she saw the "blue-steel beauty," the "blaster."

She opened the door for him, swung the seat back forward. Grebb put the suitcase in back and settled beside her, the gun on his lap.

She started the car with a lurch that shook them.

"Calm down! If they were around, they'd have made their move."

She put the car smoothly in motion, her attention nervously divided between driving and what he was doing with the gun on his lap. It clicked and he pulled something out of the handle.

"What are you doing?"

"Checking the clip, making sure it's loaded. These .45s are blasters when you know how to handle 'em. But if you don't get your finger off the trigger, the damned thing spills its whole guts, fires the whole clip before you can stop it. If you don't watch it, it'll yank your arm up till you're shooting the sky."

"If it's that dangerous, put it away, please!"

"Safety's on. This little button right here." He aimed the gun at her, squeezed the trigger and laughed. "Safe. Perfectly safe."

They had reached the road. She came to a stop, looked at him blankly. "If you're going to play that way . . ."

"I'm not playing!" he said with sudden venom. "I figure they would have made their move by now; I figure they don't have any line on me. But there's another way to figure. There's a telephone right there—" he thumbed toward the motel office—" and a gunshot around *here* would bring the cops fast." He broke off grimly. "Get moving! I think we're all right. But just in case." He patted the gun.

She was driving at only thirty or thirty-five miles an hour when she saw in the rear-view mirror that a sports car was nosing out of the motel grounds onto the road. She rechecked the mirror seconds later. The sports car had evidently turned in the other direction since its headlights didn't show. The Desert Ship was one of the last of the motels reaching out from the Reno-Sparks area; beyond, there was at the moment no traffic and few houses, none lighted at this time of night.

She was a mile beyond the lights of the motel when she flicked another glance at the rear-view mirror. She blinked, squinted, her heartbeat suddenly wild. Her throat choked and she couldn't speak.

She hit Grebb's arm, pointed to the rear and at the same time accelerated, making her car bolt forward. The sports car was back there in her wake, running without lights, and creeping up on her. The deadly stealth of the maneuver was terrifying, and even more frightening was the sudden brilliance of headlights the instant she kicked up her speed.

"Hit it hard," Grebb ordered. "Cut over to the center of the road. Don't let them pass."

"Yes," she said numbly, watching the speedometer hopelessly as it hit sixty, then sixty-five, because she knew the car's limitations and her own as a driver.

The sports car seemed to hang forty or fifty yards behind, losing no ground, gaining none, as if merely pacing them till they got farther into the desert. At seventy her car was beginning to strain. At seventy-five it began to shiver and the roadbed began to pound at it.

She hit a pit, jolting them so hard she thought an axle would break, and then the road curved and at that speed the

126

pull was frightening and she began to feel her hands cramping on the wheel. The sports car's droning engine sounded smooth and powerful with ample reserve. Her speedometer needle touched and quivered beyond the eighty mark on a long downgrade, and then the road began to rise steadily and her speed dropped like a slow seeping away of her own strength and every ounce of her engine power was being used and she found herself tightly straining every muscle in her body and staring at the crest of the long rise grimly, as if once there and over the top she could outrun the other car.

The next dip was shallower and the next rise steeper, and on beyond the dark, rolling hills were endless. There was not a light to be seen, except for brief, distant glimmers.

Behind her a spotlight with a brilliant beam flashed on and began to swing from side to side in a deliberate effort to harass her.

The sports car began to close the gap and Grebb shouted: "Cut over to the center!"

She eased over and then for a mile downhill the sports car was almost on her bumper, the spotlight filling her car blindingly, one of its headlights raking along her side of the car. She kept easing over to the left and then to the right but it was no use, no use at all, her car was shaking to pieces, while the solid little sports car probably hadn't begun to use its real power.

She was too far to the left side of the road and suddenly the sports car came up on her right and ran abreast of her, holding her crowded dangerously near the ragged left edge of the road, and although the terrain wasn't yet mountainous there was a definite drop-off.

Grebb was staring down through his side window. There were two men in the car. The one in the right seat was holding a rifle and motioning with it.

"What does he mean?" Ava cried shrilly.

"He means stop. So start to slow down. They'll pace us and at this range, if you can hold a smooth straight course I can pick off the rifleman first shot. . . . The instant I fire, gun this bus because when I knock off the driver their car will go wild and we want it in back of us. Hold as straight a course as you can. Start giving them evidence we're going to stop."

She slackened speed gradually. Grebb turned on the seat and, watching the men in the other car closely, bellowed out the window: "WE'RE STOPPING. . . . I AIN'T PACKING A ROD. . . ." As proof he raised both hands, empty.

She watched the road, dropping their speed. The other car stayed on their flank as if bolted to them. Grebb continued to look out the window, nodding at the men. One of his hands was on the gun. She was aware of his bringing it up, slowly, slowly, until it was at the level of the window opening.

Suddenly there were two . . . three . . . six—she couldn't count—whip cracks and roaring detonations of sound and shattering glass and Grebb's shoulder smashed into her as he fell across the seat, his head bloody, the gun thudding to the floor. She shrieked and tried to throw his weight off. Her car went out of control and over the embankment, and began to roll.

The car roof smashed thunderously against stone and there was a crumpling, tearing sound and the sky looked like the end of a spinning barrel and Grebb's dead weight was mashing against her and in the next instant she and he both pitched to the other side of the car.

Finally the car stopped upright on sloping ground and rocked and settled on its springs. There was a single tinkle of a piece of glass falling on the hood, then silence. The creaking tick-tick of sound from the cooling engine cut into her dazed senses. In an instant there would be an explosion, a wall of flame. She plunged her hand to the ignition, turned the key. Her head jerked toward the road. The sports car was parked up there and the two men in it were coming down the slope, reaching out with the long, pale beam of a flashlight.

She pawed around on the floor till she found the cold, blue-steel .45 automatic, then tried to open her door. It wouldn't budge! The warp and twist of the accident had frozen the door into the frame. Even if she could get past Grebb's bulk and out the other door, she'd be stepping right into sight of those two killers. She cried out with fright and exasperation and hurled her weight uselessly against the door, then surged up and almost literally dove out through the window opening. She picked herself up and scurried down the rough slope, crouching low like an animal.

The ground was uneven and studded with boulder masses and floored with loose, small rocks. She darted behind one boulder and the next, flinging brief, terrified glances behind her. The land rose and dipped without pattern, but she was certain that they managed to trail her unerringly by the sound she made as her shoes scuffed and dislodged small stones. Mostly the flashlight focused on her car, but now and then it seemed to nip her heels. Yet, she finally realized, the light didn't remain near her and it was possible that they were concerned with their own footing and heard little but the noise they themselves made.

They reached her car and Ava stopped, flattening herself behind a four-foot chunk of solid stone, and caught her breath, wetting her lips repeatedly. She peered cautiously over the top of the boulder, tense and listening. She was probably a short city block away from them but their voices in the thin, dry air were distinct.

"There's the son-of-a-bitch . . . lookit him! It's the best I ever seen him look. Dead. Where's the bitch?"

"She must've got thrown out."

"No, she didn't get thrown. She went out under her own steam . . . with the dough. She can't be far!"

"Gimme that flashlight. I'll get her."

"Wait a minute . . . he's got a money belt on."

She waited, listened, heard nothing for minutes. They were probably taking the money. Then they would go away, they would go away.

"Well, it's all on him. Think there's any use to take care of the bitch?"

"Hell, yes! Let's get her."

The flashlight was turned on again and its tiny white eye stared directly at her and she dropped out of view, feeling suffocated, her heartbeat suddenly out of control again. Not that they could have seen her at the distance, but . . . She cringed, waiting for them to find her, to kill her.

She stared at the dark, heavy gun she had been carrying. Remembering with dread what Grebb had said about its ungovernable deadliness, she had kept her finger away from that trigger. He had fired it once or twice, she was sure, the safety button must be in the right position for firing. . . . She shook her head, almost more frightened of it than of the murderous rifle stalking her.

They were coming closer. She could hear the scuff and scrabble of rocks rolling under their shoes, and the beam of their flashlight touched the surrounding boulders like flashes of silent lightning from a distant summer storm.

Now the distance was narrowing, the brightness of the light increasing and eventually they must reach her.

Ava was aware with an abrupt, cold chill that the beam of light had stopped, settled motionless on the boulder concealing her. The light stayed there, unwavering, as if one of them had stopped, while perhaps the other one had moved off in a flanking direction. . . .

She listened, not breathing, her mouth open, her eyes rounded. Her eyes felt raw. She blinked, listened. Yes, there it was—a tick-scuff of loose rock from somewhere off to the right. Light flooded the face and sides of the boulder hiding her; and its glow was sufficient to silhouette her for anyone observing from the side. She thought she would scream. She did scream. But surprisingly the sound articulated itself into distinct, shrill words.

"That flashlight makes a damned good target!"

"She hasn't got a gun," one of them shouted, but the flashlight snapped off.

"I can still see you," she called. "Come a little closer. See if I've got a gun. See if I can sharpshoot here the way I can on a roulette wheel. Come on, come on! I'm right behind one of these boulders. Move closer if you want to be dead. Or else back off fast!"

She heard a footstep off to the right—he was the one who had shouted, the one with the rifle, not the flashlight. Then she heard nothing. She couldn't see either of them. Minutes passed and nothing happened. Her eyes adjusted to the starlight, and out there in front of her was a small army of men crouched and prone and she knew that they were really boulders and unevennesses of the ground and rough shrubs, but among them were two living, stalking men.

Then she saw a distinct motion, a man's figure creeping forward directly in front of her concealment, within thirty feet. . . .

She eased her finger in against the dangerous trigger and aimed down at the creeping silhouette and fired. The gun kicked back and spat flame, then yanked upward and fired itself twice before she could stop it.

The jolt of its action had turned her whole body a little and the roar of it bounding off the stone deafened her right ear, imbalancing and confusing all her senses. She must have snapped her teeth shut and chipped off a fragment. . . . She sucked her breath as she realized it was no tooth fragment but a fragment of stone. She dropped flat to the

130

ground as the rifle off to the right cracked again, then again, the bullet chipping rock above her. Firing the dangerous automatic had revealed her position and now, now she was dead.

She leaped upright and aimed into the dark in the direction of the sound of the rifle, knowing it was hopeless. She fired once and the gun didn't get away from her and she fired again, operating in a sort of trancelike, cold hysteria. She knew there couldn't be more than one more shot, so she just stood there, and turned the gun to her own face and looked into the muzzle and then she heard a flurry of steps and saw the dark running man and swiveled the gun in his direction and fired. He fell yelping, his rifle clattering noisily away from him.

She retreated slowly, soundlessly, concealed herself in another place and after an interval called out: "There's plenty more where that came from, if you don't get out of here."

There was an interminable wait, then one of them yelled: "If you hear us walking, we're moving away."

"I know where you're moving. Make sure you do move away," she bluffed.

She had evidently only wounded the one she'd hit, because she could hear both of them walking at different points. Finally she located both of them, moving away. They reached her car. Then she lost them. But several minutes later the sports car's lights went on. It swung around and roared off in the direction from which it had come.

It could be a trick, she thought. One of them might have stayed.

She remained strainingly alert, peering at every possible lump of rock or unevenness in the ground to make sure it wasn't a skulking man. Nothing.

She must have waited a full hour before she moved. She stepped out, at first cautiously, then boldly.

She pulled the trigger of the gun, just to make sure it was empty. It was. She wiped it clean and dropped it on the ground.

She walked back to her car. It was on its wheels. Grebb was on the ground beside it. She tried to start her car, thinking it might run after all. It didn't.

She went back to the trunk, got out of the Fourleaf uniform and into a dress and sweater. She took her suitcase and her money and went up to the road and began to walk

131

through the dark. In about an hour an Indian family in a truck came along and gave her a lift into the next town.

From there she got a local bus, and then another. By next evening she was in Salt Lake City. When, next day, she took the plane east she had another name and her hair was short and brunette.

She stayed a week in Chicago. When she was finally on her way to Bascom City and Dave, she had a .38 caliber revolver and a box of shells.

Thirteen

The enervating, thick, wet heat of mid-August lay over Bascom City like a poultice sucking out her vitals. Ava sat inertly on a bench at the northwest edge of Hilltop Park, a nibbled peanut butter and cracker sandwich in one limp hand, her other hand half-grasping a pair of binoculars.

Late evening sunlight on the lenses of her horn-rim glasses seemed to render her eyeless and touched her thin, drawn face like fever. Her hair was cropped close to her skull and dyed black and she was not even familiar to herself any more. Under the pale-blue sundress, scattered with crumbs, the swelling of her stomach had risen clear to her diaphragm. From time to time she lifted the binoculars and brought into focus the patio area of a handsome sandstone and glass house on the far side of the golf course below.

Once, Dave in a chef's hat and patio apron turned toward her holding out a steak on a long fork and she thought there might be funny sayings on the apron and though Dave was diminished to three-quarters of an inch and she couldn't read them, she laughed sociably, measuring out a "Ha" and a "Ha" in two distinct syllables. She lowered the binoculars and took a bite of cracker, faintly amused at the notion that she was joining the meal there in the Sunday evening patio party. The first party they'd had there since the arrival two weeks ago of David Andrew McKettrick, II.

A little cramp made Ava lean forward and hold her breath and then she looked at her watch. It was eight-thirty.

She'd had a cramp at twelve-thirty just after she had got up —then at two-thirty, four-thirty, six-thirty. The regularity might mean her labor was beginning.

She finished the cracker sandwich, brushed her fingers and stood up, smoothing her skirt. She put the binoculars into her wicker basket along with her purse and the .38 revolver and began the slow walk to the other side of the park. The walk was pleasant, past tennis courts and children's swings and sandboxes and slides, and the mothers on the benches seeing her condition smiled warmly and she returned their feeling gratefully.

She paused at the far side of the park and looked out over the downtown area and beyond to the lines of freight cars and dirty old red-brick factory buildings by the river which, once the lifeblood of a colorful town, now ran with the dull city's pollution. Her gaze focused on the clean, geometric group of cement-block buildings forming the new branch factory where Dave, unencumbered now, had achieved the important assistant branch managership. She had often trained her binoculars on the modernistic glass building housing the offices, hoping to see Dave in the world which claimed his first loyalties. She thought that if once she might glimpse him there alone in a moment of brooding or regret or even memory, her heart would melt and she would be spared this alien thing that vied with the life in her belly. But she had never managed to see him there.

She began the easy, winding descent to the street, and the lower she went, the heavier and hotter and stiller the air became. She had seen him a hundred times in these past two months; often in hotel lobbies where he had ordinarily been on the move within a group of company and city officials, coming to or from a luncheon or banquet. She had seen him distantly on the golf course and at the country club, and closely several times in his picture window or yard of an evening when she walked past. She had seen him in news photos, with and without his wife, in the company of local society people or with the mayor or other leading political and business people. She had been at a nearby table on several occasions when he was dining, and within touch of him in the lobby of the Little Theater playhouse and he had not known her.

She had often seen his wife, not only with Dave, but on the downtown streets with three and four women friends, and on these occasions Ava would join the edge of their group, perhaps having lunch at a nearby table or shopping for maternity clothes or layettes. Her name, quaintly, was Verna. Her elbows were sharp as was her nose and she had high, narrow ears and a precise, firm voice. There was a general air about her of marching through life and it had seemed remarkable to Ava that her pregnant belly had been ovoid instead of boxlike.

Ava took a bus from the park to her rooming house and as she had feared the landlady was on the porch waiting for her.

"Well, did you find another place?"

"No."

"I've told you, Mrs. Davis—" she always accented the "Mrs." with crude irony to assure Ava that she didn't believe in the existence of a husband on overseas duty— "I'm not set up to accommodate children. Especially new babies."

"I'll have a place before we have to worry about that."

"You're as close to term as I ever saw a woman and I've seen plenty of them in your shape."

"Do you want me to leave tonight?"

"I'm just reminding you. You're paid for three more days. I won't take another week's rent."

She had a front corner room on the second floor and though windows were open on two walls the air was like held breath. She drew a small armchair up to the edge of the bed and went over and got packages out of the bureau drawers and brought them to the bed and sat down. She began her nightly ritual of counting every item of supply and clothing she had bought for her forthcoming baby. The ritual was slow and it was joyless, because somehow these fragile things, these reachings for a future, had no substance, no assurance. Tonight it was just too hot, and midway through she sat back and let her arms drop leadenly.

She dozed and woke sharply and sat upright, her eyes bulging as a muscular wave caught at her stomach. She stared at the clock. It was only ten. If the labor had really begun, if those cramps at two-hour intervals were the sign, and this one had come in an hour and a half instead of two hours . . .

She got up and walked around, holding herself.

Yes. He had come to her. Dave had come to her while he

134

was on his very honeymoon with that other woman. This child, *this one*, was his true issue!

When she lay quietly, very quietly, she could hear the heartbeat, the tiny other heartbeat. . . . She got up and hurried to the little stack of books she'd accumulated, four of them on pregnancy and birth problems, all of course by doctors, so there was no need for a personal doctor. Besides she was afraid to go to any person in an official capacity of any sort.

Because after all she *was* wanted—wanted for questioning about Grebb's death. Not that she'd be accused. The Chicago papers had been full of the story for several days and they had named her. The local paper had carried the story once, before she came. She'd read it in the library file. She had been named. But the story was dropped after that one item. Undoubtedly because her name sullied an important local name and embarrassed the corporation. Perhaps, she thought, seeing the story of her in trouble, Dave had wished he could reach her, help her. Her mouth became bitter. She remembered the statements about her from Cliff Hamilton, reportedly injured "seriously but not critically," in those Chicago stories. Like Cliff, like Dave!

Why the hell hadn't she done it that night just after the Fourth of July holidays? She had felt the clean, hard drive and the courage in her to do it and she had taken the gun and ridden an owl bus out to Dave's neighborhood and walked to his house. She had planned to ring the bell and announce herself and gain entrance and kill him and his female and her unborn.

She had gone to the back. There had been open French doors. She had stood outside and listened to them breathing and had seen them in their separate twin beds, helpless before her. She had taken off her shoes and stepped into the room and stood as motionless as the wall. She had taken out the gun and held it in her hand and waited and watched, but she could not kill the unborn. She had felt the stirring of the child in her own belly, life protesting death. She had rushed away, terrified by her own fear more than of what she had almost done. Now the unborn was born!

And her own child was restless within her. He could feel her urgency. The next cramp seized her agonizingly; the pain was so fierce that—that—no, she wouldn't die, not yet, not yet. . . .

135

By morning the labor pains came every half-hour. She was squeezed dry of all her sweat and still she oozed moisture. She changed her clothes three times. This was it, she knew, this was it. No avoiding it, she must get to a hospital. She went down to the phone and called a cab and hurried up the stairs and got her suitcase with the things she would need. She was at the curb when the cab arrived.

"County Hospital. Hurry!"

"Oh-oh! Race with the stork?"

"Race with the stork!"

Then she was at the hospital, trying hysterically to explain to them that she *had* no local physician, that she had been en route from New York, trying to get home to Cincinnati for this. . . . Yes, yes, she could pay for three days . . . cash. . . .

One of the young house doctors came to her in the labor room where the nurses had strapped her and began to ask a lot of silly questions. She lay and rode with the violent waves of pain. She felt a flood of warm liquid and knew the sac had burst and she begged: "Give me something! I can't stand it!"

Blissfully, she was going under, and the rhythms of agony were muted, dreamlike. She floated and thought of her granddaddy and then she was in a bed and it was late evening and it was all over and she could not remember any pain. She smiled as a grave-faced nurse came in with a glass of fruit juice.

"Where's my baby?"

"Drink this, Mrs. Davis."

"Where's my *baby*?"

"Doctor is on his way."

"Yes, yes, but where's my baby? I don't even know if he's a boy. I've got to see him, you know. . . ." She began to cry, the tears rolling down her face. "Please, where is he?"

A man in a business suit, a round-faced man with steel-rim glasses, came in and smiled at her and spoke to the nurse. He turned to Ava.

"Now, my dear . . ." he began gently.

"What are you keeping from me? Was he . . . was he stillborn? He couldn't have been, because I know he was alive. He told me about it every day of his life. He kicked and he told me. I could feel his very heartbeat. . . . He's not *dead*?"

136

"I don't know if you're going to be able to sustain what I must tell you, but. . ."

And he began to tell her a horror story.

"Who are you?" she interrupted. "You don't belong in this hospital. Are you a doctor? Who are you?"

"I'm a doctor. I'm a psychiatrist."

She sat up. "I want out of here. You can't hold me. I want my clothes at once and I want out of here. I demand to be released. Do you hear me? Shall I phone a lawyer? I won't listen to you. I want out of here, do you hear me? There are lawyers and judges in my family. If I am detained in this madhouse five more minutes, I shall sue. For false imprisonment. Now if you're prepared to face that, just refuse to check me out of this place."

As to his claims that she had not given birth, had never even been pregnant, had imagined every last symptom, these were too outrageous to dignify with any discussion.

Within two hours she was walking out. It was one thing to *think* she was insane, another to prove it and have her declared. The story was already in the local paper. It didn't name her, but there it was:

"THE BABY THAT WASN'T THERE!"

She read the story, including the learned opinion of a "specialist in abnormal psychology." According to this fraud, this apologist for the murderous incompetence of the hospital, she had had what was known as a pseudo pregnancy. It was a far from unknown phenomenon.

She threw the paper away, sneering. According to that accomplice in murder, these were hysterical, often virgin women, working out some purely psychological problem. She got a cab and went out to her rooming house, laughing to herself at one of the examples cited of such a woman, who would not believe her baby had not been born and continued for years in an asylum to carry around a rolled blanket, believing that this was a live baby. Somehow, the idea seemed very funny.

She certainly didn't think that cloth was flesh, and *she* certainly *knew* that her *brain* hadn't dropped down to kick the insides of her stomach, the way her baby had kicked her. Ava grinned—the little devil! He had been a vital little devil, with a strong heart, so strong she had actually been able to hear it. An imagined baby couldn't have a heartbeat, learned professors.

137

She wondered just exactly how they had disposed of his poor, murdered little body—oh, not first-degree-murdered little body. Incompetence and negligence would be, she thought, something like manslaughter. . . . She got out of the cab at her rooming house.

She went into her room, locked the door. She went at once to the drawer where she kept her gun. It was there.

She checked. It was loaded. She put several extra cartridges in her purse. She didn't know how many it might take. Two rifle bullets had ended Grebb. It might take more revolver bullets for Dave. And for the dear, sweet mother of his living child. One would be sufficient for David Andrew McKettrick, II.

She sat and watched the clock and waited and when it was two in the morning she stirred herself and went down to the phone in the lower hall and called a cab and went outside to wait in the heavy, damp, hot air and then she got into the cab and they rode and passed the golf course and Hilltop Park and then they were on the street where Dave would no longer live.

"Don't wait," she instructed the driver. "They're expecting me."

The cab waited anyhow. She went up and rang the bell and in a minute the porch light and a hall light went on simultaneously and she waved at the cabby and he drove off and then she put her hand into her purse and held it there, gripping the gun.

"Yes? Who is it?" It was Dave, peering out from a two-way panel of glass through which he could see her and she couldn't see him.

"Ava," she said distinctly. She had removed her glasses. Even with short black hair he couldn't totally fail to recall her face. "I'm in trouble; I must see you. I'm desperate."

He opened the door, wearing pajama pants and a robe. His hair was tousled; a half-torpid bafflement spread over his broad, handsome face. His face had filled out somewhat, with a beginning trace of pomposity in the angle of his chin and the flesh of his jowls. She stepped in and stood, looking him up and down, a half-smile on her mouth.

"How smug and safe you look, Dave. To be a small nut in a machine certainly gives a man stature in his own eyes, doesn't it? What does it feel like? Does it feel like genuine importance?"

He looked at her disapprovingly. "What do you want?"

"I want you to turn around and march back to your woman and your kid, and I want you to do it promptly, just as if someone in the hierarchy had sent you a memo instructing you to turn and move away from me."

"What the devil's wrong with you?"

She smiled tightly and pulled the gun out of the purse. She looked at him and said nothing and watched his cautious mind working, deciding to humor her. He turned around and started along the central hall. Ava followed.

"I'll shoot you in the back," she said calmly, "if you make any sudden move. Remember I'm not a proper corporation person, therefore there are no angles to what I say. I speak true. I will shoot you six times in the back before you hit the floor if you try anything. Be sure you lead me into the proper bedroom."

"Dave, what is it?" a woman called from a room ahead.

Dave didn't answer, but turned into the bedroom. Verna was sitting up and the bed lamp was on, and a few feet away was the crib where their living creature slept.

"This is my ex-wife. She's in a nasty mood and she's got a gun."

"It's perfectly ridiculous. She can't bluff me," Verna said, glaring and reaching for the bedside phone as Ava came in.

Ava stopped and placed her feet apart and sighted the gun as it instructed in the manual. She squeezed the trigger, taking out the slack gently, just as in her dry-firing practice, and the gun fired.

The sudden, high volume of sound was stunning, and the tiny spot that appeared at the base of Verna's throat was amazing. It works, Ava thought, wanting to laugh. She angled the gun upward slightly and fired again and this time the explosion was followed by a neat third eye an inch above and midway between Verna's original two. Smiling, Ava pulled the trigger again and again, one of the shots entering Verna's breast, the other her cheek. If Mrs. Dave Number Two wasn't dead she would be soon.

Dave stood almost paralyzed, his jaw dropped, his eyes widening incredulously. Verna didn't fall off the bed. She just sagged on back against the pillow and Dave whispered: "My God, Ava. My God!"

The baby began to scream and Ava pointed the gun toward the crib and Dave suddenly sprang toward her. She swiveled easily and backstepped, the gun swinging around toward him, holding level.

He froze. He wet his lips and the blood drained out of his face as he mumbled: "The baby . . . the baby's scared. . . . Sweetheart, you don't want to hurt the *baby*. Let me take him up and stop his crying."

"That won't save you. I came here to kill you. I'm going to kill you. Go on and pick him up if you want to and I'll shoot through him."

"Ava . . . you're not like that. . . . What's wrong?"

"What *is* wrong? Or what was wrong? It was my tongue. It lacked the flair for boot licking."

For the first time his dark face twisted into life for her, as he pleaded, "I loved you, Ava, and a part of me always will. You loved me, and a part of you always will. This is a terrible thing, a dreadful thing. Think of your granddaddy, Ava. It would break his heart to see you a killer."

"I hate you, Dave You're a crawing slime of a man, with your smug, high-priced obedience. You let them buy your private life and select your woman! You're not going to reap any more reward for it. You're dead, you're an owned creature, not a man. For another woman, for any decent personal reason, I could have forgiven you for killing me! But you have no respect for yourself."

She fired and he seized his chest and fell, crying out. And she fired again down at his head. There were no more shells in the gun and she calmly reloaded and fired into his worthless, slave head three more times.

And then, with three bullets left, she walked to the crib and told the screaming baby, "You'd sell your freedom, too; you'd betray everything a man lives by. I'll save you from that."

She held the little head in one hand and pressed the gun muzzle gently into the softness of the unformed skull.

And then the tears began to flow down her cheeks and she lifted the crying child in her arms.

She held him to her breast, crooning in a sweet voice, and it was there she stood, oblivious of all the lost world, when the police broke in.

The End

"What You Need Is A Boy Friend"

Ava stared in shocked fascination at the sheer brute strength of the man who'd forced his way into her life—and her Reno apartment. She knew Grebb was a muscle man for the Syndicate. Yet his very evil excited her.

She shook her head, shuddering at the thought of any other lover than her husband—no matter how brutally Dave had used her. "I couldn't go through with it . . . I—I'd get sick."

"You're already sick." Grebb tapped his head. "But I thought you had possibilities."

. . . She almost fainted when he struck her. Then a wild excitement coursed through her and she feverishly clutched at his coat. "Stay with me," she moaned. "Stay . . ."

AUTHOR'S PROFILE

A Mid-Westerner by birth, Stuart Friedman has seen most of America in his travels and now lives in San Francisco.

Among the various activities that have occupied his time are, selling advertising, working with a foundry maintenance gang, selling real estate and the operation of a labor-industry counselling service.

He turned to writing as a career in 1938 and his first published book was a well-received history of Indiana. Subsequently, he switched to fiction and has made many sales to leading national magazines. His books include the two current Monarch bestsellers, THE WAY WE LOVE and THE REVOLT OF JILL BRADDOCK.